D1077432

White Chappell Scarlet Tracings

Iain Sinclair has lived in London for thirty years. In the 1970s he ran Albion Village Press, publishing Brian Catling, Chris Torrance and several volumes of his own poetry. He is the author of two other novels: *Downriver*, which won the 1992 Encore Award for the year's best second novel, and the James Tait Black Memorial Prize; and *Radon Daughters*. He has also published several books of poetry, including *Lud Heat* and *Suicide Bridge*. His most recent books are the critically acclaimed *Lights Out for the Territory*, a record of journeys on foot around London, and *Slow Chocolate Autopsy*, a collection of linked stories illustrated by Dave McKean.

ALSO BY IAIN SINCLAIR

Fiction
Downriver
Radon Daughters
Slow Chocolate Autopsy (with Dave McKean)

Non-fiction
Lights Out for the Territory

Documentary
The Kodak Mantra Diaries (Allen Ginsberg in London)

Poetry
Black Garden Poems
Muscat's Würm
The Birth Rug
Flesh Eggs & Scalp Metal: Selected Poetry
Jack Elam's Other Eye
Penguin Modern Poets 10
The Ebbing of the Kraft
Conductors of Chaos (Editor)

Iain Sinclair

WHITE CHAPPELL SCARLET TRACINGS

Granta Books

London

Granta Publications, 2/3 Hanover Yard, London N1 8BE

First published in Great Britian by Goldmark 1987
This edition published by Granta Books 1998

A CIP catalogue record for this book is available from the British Library.

1 3 5 7 9 10 8 6 4 2

Printed and bound in Great Britain by Mackays of Chatham plc

".. then I tell you what change I think you had better begin with, grandmother. You had better change Is into Was and Was into Is, and keep them so."

"Would that suit your case? Would you not be always in pain then?" asked the old man tenderly.

"Right!" exclaimed Miss Wren with another chop.

for
B. Catling, there before me
and
Martin Stone, always ahead

book one

MANAC

1

THERE IS an interesting condition of the stomach where ulcers build like coral, fibrous tissue replacing musculature, cicatrix dividing that shady receptacle into two zones, with communication by means of a narrow isthmus: a condition spoken of, with some awe, by the connoisseurs of pathology as "hour glass stomach".

Waves of peristalsis may be felt as they pass visibly across the upper half of the abdomen, left to right, as if conscious of diurnal etiquette. Friends of surgeons have watched mesmerised, gawping, with the empty minded rapture of plein-air sunset smudgers, at this revelation of secret tides. A boring pain recurs, beaks in the liver, even the thought of food becomes a torture; a description that starts at discomfort is refined with each meal taken until it colonises the entire consciousness, then copious vomiting, startling to casual observers, brings relief.

Nicholas Lane, excarnate, hands on severely angled knees, stared out across the dim and featureless landscape, then dropped his gaze to the partly-fermented haddock, mixed with mucus, that poured from his throat, that hooked itself, bracken coloured, over the tough spears of roadside grass. Lumps, that were almost skin, split and fell to the ground. New convulsions took him: his bones rattled with their fury. Patches of steaming bouillabaisse spilled a shadow pool across the thin covering of snow.

'Toads!' remarked Dryfeld, ignoring the event, 'the females carry the males on their backs across these roads. Or die in the attempt. Like Shetland fisherwomen. Wet skirts tucked into their belts. Out through the breakers. Husbands. Drinking all night. Cling to their necks.'

He broke off, scribbled a few lines into his ring folder, in stiff blue capitals; then, unprompted, relaunched his monologue.

'If the A1 had anticipated itself, Darwin would never have needed to leave these shores. It's all here, Monsieur. Only the fittest and most insanely determined life forms can battle across that river of death to reach the central reservation – but then, ha! They are free from predators. They live and breathe under the level of the fumes. They stay on this grass spine, leave the city, or the sea-coast, escape, feral cats and their like, and travel the country, untroubled, north to south. The lesser brethren die at the verges. And are spun from our wheels, flung to the carrion. Grantham's daughter, this is your vision!

And when the cities are finished, abandoned, life will steal back in down this protected tongue. The new world will evolve *here*.'

Nicholas Lane's stomach having emptied itself he climbed back into the car, found that he still had one cigarette stashed, called for a match. Nobody had one. He sniffed, drew his hand across his nose, and left the cigarette dangling like a piece of torn lip.

To call him thin would be to underdescribe him. His skin was damp paper over bone. Nothing could get into his intestine so he functioned directly on head energy. An icicle of pure intelligence.

The mid-England dark, torpid and thick, a kind of willed ignorance, was wide about them. A heavy but sluggish motorcar facing south, mudded hubs, filthy windows. The kind of car that is common in the antiques game, strong enough to take plenty of potential Welsh dressers. Not so common in the book trade. See one and you see a villain. Call it a Volvo. A case of sealed heats, old smoke, sweats, bags, fears, papers, coffee nerves, sleepless, questing, never willing to call it a day.

They had spent a gentle half-week motoring from London to Glasgow, to Stirling, to Edinburgh, to Newcastle, to Durham, with brief expeditions to Carlisle, Richmond, Ripon and many lesser centres, many a rumour chased, and after nothing more interesting than used books.

The car was indeed filled with them. Elephant folios, loose, sets of bindings, sold by the yard, carrier bags of explosive paperbacks, first editions packed into cardboard boxes, leaflets on fireworks, golf novels, needlework patterns, catalogues of light fittings, vegetarian tracts, anything that could be painlessly converted into money, so that they could get back out on the road again.

Jamie, known to many an auction ring as "the Old Pretender", was at the wheel, for it was his car, asleep, his near horizontal forehead sunk onto his arm. Septic skin, a tropical pallor, old planting family, liver already counted out, and suffering a slightly inconvenient dose of the clap. Useful man. Plenty of relatives with decayed mansions, inhabited by domestic animals and uncontrolled vermin. Be lucky to see his thirtieth birthday. When he wasn't drunk, he was asleep. And he had not, as yet, been allowed his sundowner; Dryfeld would not permit the car to halt in daylight, until the threat of a lapful of Nicholas Lane's week-old breakfast, and the vision, across the road, of a phonebox, gave him pause.

Dryfeld sported a camelhair coat, with lumps of the camel still attached, more padded horse-blanket than coat: it was stretched well beyond its limits in accommodating the dealer's rigid shoulders. His weight seemed all to have been compressed somewhere near the top of his spine, he had no neck. His skull was shaven, deathrow chic, and was so massive and burdened with unassimilated information that it tipped aggressively forward, almost onto his chest. He hunched his shoulders so that they could support the weight, striding at reckless speed, taken for a hunchback. The thick skin of his face stretched into a permanent frown.

It was tragic that Max Beckmann died too soon to have a crack at him: the darkest self-portraits hint at something of Dryfeld's flavour. But Dryfeld never posed, was never at rest.

His pockets sagged, tormented by the selection of coins needed for his hourly phone-calls. His business was all done through other people's premises. He would ring his contacts day or night, from every caff, or garage, or railway station where he found himself with a crack of time. So that when he arrived back in London he could immediately pick up more money, cash in his cheques, drop a sack of recent purchases, and leave again.

He lived nowhere, was nobody. Made it his business to stay out of all the files, lists, electoral rolls. He took his name, and he had only one, from St Mary Matfellon, Whitechapel. The promise of an anarchist booksale in Angel Alley had drawn them into the labyrinth, but the sale, being run by anarchists, was naturally cancelled and moved, unannounced, to another location, at another time, changed from books to records. The moment was not to be wasted. Dryfeld plunged into the Whitechapel Library and stormed through the accounts of the eliminated church. Among the list of rectors he found, *Tho. Dryfeld, 10 January 1503 – 2 March 1512*. Nobody was using the name, it became his.

He was as well read as any railway cleaner with his pick of the first class carriages, pockets bulging with slightly corrupted newsprint, thick ink-stained fingers. He absorbed all the information by touch, a kind of idiot's braille.

Nicholas Lane never read a newspaper, carried no cash. Paid for his tea with a crumpled cheque. He appeared as frail as Dryfeld was meaty. But it was an illusion. He hopped about like a stick insect, at a speed inconceivable to mere mammals. You could be talking to him on the street only to find, in mid sentence, that he had shot off at a tangent, down a side alley, across a road, into a bookshop that looked to all other eyes like a hair-salon or a boot mender's.

ʰ had a radar that was unequalled. Black skintight trousers
  ᵧing thin ankles in white socks, Brick Lane shoes, sharp

as chisel points, a bargain, if his feet had been two sizes smaller. Beret, like a fruit-bat, his familiar, always on his head: nobody had ever seen him without it. Subterranean visionary. In this context the word genius could be applied without any fear of hyperbole. Brilliant possession of the martyred self.

A nasal grunt from Jamie, as if he had swallowed his tongue and not much cared for the taste. Broken-down grouse assassin, his plate-sized lenses so smeared and greasy that a pilot with 20/20 vision would have been white-sticked by them. Book ripper, bladesman, rapidly slicing the views, costumes, maps, gutting the colour or polishing the leatherware: books into furniture. Fuelled on whisky. Hands shaking on the wheel of sleep. Groaning. Tremens. Quite justified.

The narrator, feeling posthumous, thought of himself as the Late Watson. The secret hero who buries his own power in the description of other men's triumphs. Dangerous ground. Flickering between modesty and blasphemy. Pinched into the co-driver's seat, boxes and maps across his knees, polo-sucking, costive owl, built around a now firmly packed gut, cemented in guilt, involuntary retention of oat cake, porridge, turnip, energy trapped, red eye lidless with coffee, unable, away from home, to do anything more than break wind. Hair of the dog scratching at his scalp.

Dryfeld strode back from the phonebox, fists pounding at the driver's window, cardiac flutter. Nine o'clock, an early December evening, black snow, his breath making frantic cartoons in the air; Mossy Noonmann would see us. He never closes to the trade. Or opens to the public. Who have been known to faint, gasp or curse, at the first sight of one of his pricings. He took a quiet pleasure, sucking wet lipped at his pipe stem, watching the innocents drop the book and try to get to the door before he could spear them with his ancient mariner eye, stone-fix them, stand casually across the door space, driving them back into the paperback shelves where they can make a token purchase of a few pounds and escape into the sunlight.

Nicholas Lane ran a line of badly adulterated Bolivian snuff across the top of his briefcase, rolled up a returned cheque, and took it in the nostril. Hammered the mucous membrane. Hit the brain jelly with a white dart. His eyes sharpened, his already twitching and prehensile fingers played with the combination of his lock, a soothing sequence of power-inducing numbers. Look out, Mossy.

The four horsemen were outside Steynford, and they were about to take the town.

*

Mossy Noonmann's bookshop, if we afford it the courtesy of that title, was probably the only one open in the whole of the Midlands, from Wolverhampton to Boston, and out into the North Sea. And he was the least likely proprietor. How he had come here nobody knew and few cared to guess.

He stood, stooping, a few inches under the low ceiling of his ill-lit empire; lacquered in dry sweat, glistening. He had found a role to suit his height and he was quite prepared to play it. He affected the trappings of the trade as they might have been described in a 1930s detective novel: an unruly pipe, the stem almost bitten away, sucked, spat through, poked at, scraped, cleaned into the filthiest stick of tar, unlit, and frequently pocketed in a condemned floral waistcoat. His face had a shocked and naked quality, as if it had been covered for years in a helmet of hair and then suddenly, and judicially, exposed to the light. His skull was heavy, water-filled, and tended to come to rest on one or other of his shoulders.

It was impossible to believe that the stock in his shop had been selected with any notion of trading in it. It was as if every other dealer within fifty miles had been allowed to tip one sack of their most leprous and flaky dogs onto his floor. The shelves, being decent timber, had long ago been sold. There were typed cards announcing LITERATURE, PHILOSOPHY, POST-CARDS, CRIME, MOVIE STARS, WAR, FASHION; but these, having been so laboriously produced, were dropped anywhere, two good ideas in one day was too much to cope with, and the cards now bore no relation whatever to the heaps on which they lay.

Mossy had trouble breathing. He was not convinced that the rewards repaid the effort. He took breath in, but after that let it fend for itself. He groaned. This had a somewhat un-centring effect on humans reaching for a copy of, say, Winwood Reade's *The Martyrdom of Man*. They tended then not so much to drop the books they were holding as to throw them across the room, adding to the already generous measure of confusion.

Mossy's nose was a thing to be admired. He admired it. He looked after it better than he looked after his family. He would pick at the lining with a match-stick, roll out an interesting lump, either of skin or of snot, even food, then gasp for breath after his exertions. He would mop himself with a shirt-sized handkerchief. Perhaps it was a shirt; it must have been a very old one. He was the only person to find Steynford tropical. He dripped with the effort of striking a match and let it burn out in his fingers.

Most of Mossy's business had once been transacted on the telephone, until that instrument had been cut off. Literally. Mossy took his pocket-knife to the cord and severed it, tying a ticket to the bone. It was a realistic view. Everything has its price-tag and it might as well be visible.

Now Mossy took to appearing at Auction Houses; he haunted the rooms, watching the bidders, selecting a likely novice with a nervous arm, and begging a lift, 'just up the road'. The road being the A1. His benefactor, in a state of hysterical paralysis, was persuaded to chauffeur Mossy to the very door of his shop. Then to enter, to carry in a box. The fact that it was the driver's own box seemed always to be overlooked. The order of release could only be obtained by purchasing a decent heap of cover-less odd volumes and first editions with additional printing histories thoughtfully erased, scarce issues put out by Book Clubs. It was always when Mossy threatened to brew up a large mug of coffee that the cheque books appeared and another neophyte was broken in.

Noonmann was a New Yorker, veteran of Peace Eye Bookstore, who, not fancying an engagement in South East Asia in the mid-60s, had returned to the Europe of his forefathers by way of Liverpool, then, briefly, the centre of the Universe. A single evening disproved this conceit: Noonmann found a mattress in Westbourne Grove. There were minor misunderstandings over rent books, social security paperwork, import/export regulations concerning self-administered resins from the Middle East; there was a misplaced briefcase of ounces, and Mossy decided to hit the road.

Two hours up the A1 and the Camberwell-domiciled holder of a Heavy Goods Vehicle Licence was ready to turn it in rather than carry Mossy another mile. He walked down the hill into Steynford. He's been there ever since, and never walked so far again.

*

Jamie let the car roll silently down the main street, the Pelican Hotel on his left, passing it, with only the faintest and most wistful of sighs. A cheese-coloured town, slicked over with fen sleet, damp as an abattoir coldstore, distinguished by a profusion of moulting snail-horn churches, their steeples discouragingly set with sharks' teeth. Over the river, a touch on the power-steering brings them into the yard adjoining Mossy Noonmann's shop.

Before the others have got the doors open Jamie has been into the shop, seen that there are no books larger than tombstones, no leather left on the spines, no gilt, and he's out again, uphill, hands in pocket, scratching himself, shirt tails flying back, into a narrow passageway, up some stairs, across a deserted shopping precinct, he's never been to the place before, can smell the fermented grain inside the bottle, is ensconced in the saloon bar, coat collar up against the Lincolnshire winds that he does not trust to stay out of licensed premises, and is calling for a refill.

Mossy shifts his head from one shoulder to the other, hazarding no remark, as the others push past him, with like informality, down the step, and dive directly into separate areas of the shop. Naturally they ignore the books on the few remaining shelves, or those in what might once have been a glass-fronted cabinet – but immediately start to examine, with painstaking care, the loose sheets under tables, anything without a spine; they spill out the contents of boxes onto the floor.

'All crap', Dryfeld announces, unnecessarily.

'You guys!' Mossy remarks, world-weary, but with something of admiration in his tone. 'You fucking guys.'

He succeeded in spearing a spectacularly colourful glob of snot and prodded it across the counter. It was speckled like granite. He'd probably have it set into a signet ring.

'You're too fucking much.' He killed a bottle of room temperature Lucozade, spun open the cap on another.

Dryfeld, totally ignoring the prices inscribed in the books, which bore no relation to their value, at auction, by catalogue, or any other method of trade known to humanity, started to put a heap of "possibles" on the counter, "for negotiation." He's quite prepared to talk it through to dawn; or until the first shop opens in Hendon. Or until Mossy's screaming cells demand another anodyne fix. Whoever talked about getting high hadn't met Mossy. He absorbed, sweated, continued. He looked like an ill-shaved bison but he had a will that could only be measured in geological time. His stock might need carbon dating, but he wouldn't crack.

First edition dealers are interested in nothing but condition, they couldn't care less about the title or the contents so long as the book is fine, mint, untouched, intact, a second time virgin: they wouldn't have a prayer here.

But Nicholas Lane is resilient, he starts to work through a mess of *Horner's Penny Stories for the People*, so well-tanned they're oven ready; pausing to examine one copy closely. He hasn't blinked since they got out of the car: his pupils enlarge by a couple more points. He snatches up the whole pile, putting them under his arm. Then rapidly selects a hand of terminally distressed Austin Freemans, a "Lost Race" yarn, lacking front free endpaper, a romance set in Burma, and a Jonathan Latimer paperback for his own use. Nicholas Lane and Dryfeld were remarkable figures in the book trade: they could both read, a book a day, between shops. The speed of Lane's decisions was breathtaking and those who know him will recognise that he has made a find. All of the other choices are wrapping paper and can be painlessly junked.

The Late Watson is somewhat languid. The shop looks uncomfortably like a diagram of his stomach. He began to hallucinate. The room extended into the dreadnought hulk of Ripon Cathedral. It was raining, or the roof was melting. The pews were stacked with untitled proof copies, a thousand to every row, and somewhere in amongst them Graham Greene's own copy, the original version, of *Brighton Rock*, with all the period racism not yet expurgated. He needed to run his head under a tap. He blundered through the main body of the shop, up some steps, into the back room.

The bowl of the lavatory was filled with painted female faces. Titles like *Blue Blood Flows East, Lady – Don't Turn Over*, floated sodden on the surface. The Science Fiction titles were spread over the floor, along with a good supply of used and unused needles. Crunch across them, like walking on locusts. There is no light, he has a torch in his pocket, ready for winter morning markets, for nipping into forbidden cellars and peeping through the keyholes of locked rooms. Spots a tolerable copy of *The Anubis Gates* by Tim Powers, published 1985 at £9.95 and modestly marked up by Mossy to £15. That's ok. He can get £40 for it. Picks up half a dozen others to jettison when they negotiate. Back to the shop, one sleeper, an inscribed copy of Peter Ackroyd's *Hawksmoor* for a fiver: which brings him up to his day's target.

The sole advantage of Mossy's shop is that he does not offer coffee to dealers. This form of politeness has wrecked more stomachs than the combined forces of all the fast food dead-chicken combos.

'You're putting me on, man. This lot comes to £238 – I'm saying you can have them for £210. Two hundred. And ten. Pounds. What do you want, man, me to *give* them to you? For Chrissakes, man!'

Mossy's indignation is perfectly assumed, almost genuine. He falls back, breathless.

Dryfeld, unmoved. '£60. Best offer.'

'Get out of here! You know what they catalogue at? Are you *serious?*'

'Sixty quid. Take it or leave it.'

'I'm giving you nearly three hundred fucking quids worth of books, where else in this world are you even going to *see* these books? Giving, at £200. What you want? Bastard! You want to fuck my wife and kids as well?'

'Sixty quid.'

Mossy swills Lucozade, dribbling orange bubbles into the cleft of his chin. Shrugs, half turns, appeals to the narrator, to Nicholas Lane who is performing various self-contained operations with cigarettes, resinous shavings, and a box of Mossy's matches.

'OK, guys, back to my house. Time? You've got time. Where else is open? My house. I'll show you more stuff. Can you believe him? A fucking skinhead gorilla! £120 for three hundred pounds worth of books on fucking Red Indians, I throw in the needlework. Listen, man, don't think you can tell me anything about Indians. I took courses with Olson at Buffalo, man. The fucking Library of Congress would fly over at that price. You want me to ring them?'

He grabs the amputated telephone and shoves it in Dryfeld's face.

'Bastard still wants to fuck about. I should have killed him the last time.'

'Sixty.' Dryfeld paces, uneasy in a room without newspapers.

*

You can climb up from the river through narrow passageways, where Dryfeld's shoulders brush the algae from the damp walls, grey snow-melt leaking into Nicholas Lane's paper-thin shoes; in spasm, through the secret intestines of the town. They pass, and ignore, the slumped shadow of Jamie, a smear on the pub window, dosing himself with Jamesons and cola chasers.

Mossy Noonmann's wife is not made radiant by the prospect of her husband returning, no deal set, three half-crazed book-dealers at his heels, with their bundles of paper, their saurian determinism. The tv-set is on but the rest of the furniture has been wasted. Two small pale children of undetectable sex sit a yard from the set, not noticeably well-fed, though their un-matched pyjamas are witness to meals having been taken at some point in their recent history, involving plentiful use of the sauce bottle. Lank-haired and mute: they outstare the elec-tronic fishtank.

The wife withdraws to practise what sounds like an advanced course in arc-welding in the kitchen: the negotiations continue. Dryfeld takes out a fat roll of notes and starts counting the sixty in fivers.

'I'm asking one hundred pounds. You want to steal four hun-dred pounds worth of books, ok. Steal the fuckers. It's your karma, baby.'

Before Mossy can grab the cash his wife's hand appears, it's gone, she's gone, his performance of animation collapses, he nods out, shivers, turns down the sound on the tv; the carnage and mania is leaping in rabid cuts behind him, as if it was all escaping from just inside his eyelids. The children do not ob-ject, or move. The wife materialises once more.

'Dick-head!'

Turns the sound back up, to the top. The windows shudder. The front door has been left open and the demented yelps and barks invade the otherwise silent street.

Dryfeld packs his Smithsonian Indians into a canvas holdall, straps running underneath for extra strength, sign of the professional runner.

Nicholas Lane can sense the narrowing of the lumen of the pylorus, the first delicate, almost sensual, ripplings of pain, the foretaste of vomit in the throat, Proustian recall, Glaswegian Dal Mosola about to resurface. He goes through the palest form of argument, cutting Mossy's tenner to eight quid, agreeing a bulk price for the *Penny Stories* that anybody less desperate than Mossy would have junked to Oxfam. He makes it onto the frozen grass and sprays two or three pints of old food into an ornamental flower-bowl.

'Spewed up his ring,' thought the narrator, a phrase picked up in Walthamstow, of uncertain meaning, but strong displacement. 'Spewed up his ring.'

Recorded violence and actual violence mix, faked blows and authentic shuddering of violated flesh: they head gratefully for the car, each with his secret triumph of books.

The car is waiting for them, useless. They stand around it, unable to get in, or on; Jamie in sleep, his head upon the bar-room table.

*

The windows of the bar are mercifully frosted, keeping out all sight of the stone walls, this sandblasted town. Jamie wakes and fumbles for one of Nicholas Lane's cigarettes. He has a lighter but it doesn't work. There never was a case-hardened smoker who had a match. They measure out their days in bumming lights. Never was a true nicotine junkie who had a watch. It would be superfluous: they can weigh time in their craving for the burnt tongue, a lick of old ashtrays.

Dryfeld having flung his purchases into the holdall has no interest in examining them. He's made his phone call. They're sold. He'll have his money before dawn and be on the Penzance train by breakfast-time. A bundle of still crisp newspapers.

He starts scribbling in the ring folder. His hand writing has been accurately described as looking like "poor quality knitting." It has the advantage of being unreadable, even to him.

And though he can't do two things at once he does them so closely together that they blend into one crumb-spattered shuffle. He writes, frowning, lips moving, breaks off, devours, tears up a plate of thick-cut cheese sandwiches. The virulent orange grains of moistened cheese rolling out of the corners of his mouth, generous beads of milky spittle. Savage vegan.

The narrator's books are bagged also. And of no further interest. Once bought he'd sell them to anyone, for anything; preferably several times over. They are the stigmata of guilt, the visible sign that he remains in this tawdry profession: he does not have the spirit, yet, to be proud of these fine and active corruptions. Ancient pretensions glaze him into a sour inertia.

Nicholas Lane, concentrated, subdues the circling vortex of pain drilling into his gut; the true enthusiast. The warrior-knight who dredges up grail treasures out of the dead land, himself dying from open wounds. Gone in the teeth, but brilliant in eye and finger.

He knows that pain is life: every twist and bite flashes another synapse, a connection burns out, keeping his edge sharp. He unstrings the bundle of old papers. Throws back a brandy, hitting the ulcer wound like a shot of salt.

The first point he can reveal is that the outer wrappings bear no direct relation to the contents. A Penny Story, *Out in the Wide World* by Fannie Eden, fetching cover illustration of wistful young lady, Chatterton in drag, standing outside her attic window looking across the roofs of the city to the unfocused distance of St Paul's and the sister churches, proves on closer examination to contain two sheets of prophetic millennial rantings pasted over a remnant of the original text.

"'Master, master,' she cried out, 'there's a villain of a Jew gone up into that picture-place upstairs! He says as how the awful looking pictur' belongs to him 'cause he lent the gentleman money on it, and he is carrying it away.'

Molly started up with a cry of dismay.

'Hush, Molly, do not trouble yourself! There must be some mistake,' Dr. Maitland said. 'Stay here, and I will see this Jew fellow,' and he turned and left her."

A number of other yarns, involving tigers, boat races, abandoned waifs, bearded card-players, were left naked with no cover, no illustrations, no advertisements.

Some covers had been recklessly taped to quite alien interiors, some fixed with rubber solution into brown wrappings. But it had been the name of Beeton's Christmas Annual and the search for the magic date, 1887, that had settled the purchase for Nicholas Lane.

There were copies; but they were split and scattered. Taped into a romance by H. Fitzgerald entitled *Madeline's Temptation* was what appeared to be some version of the legendary Christmas Annual with the first printing of the first appearance of Sherlock Holmes, *A Study in Scarlet.*

The covers had gone, there were some annotations to the text. The date "1878" had been altered to "1888". The word "Nettley" had been altered to "Netley." Nicholas Lane paused to flick a globe of dry white spittle from his lips.

'At worst,' he said, 'a variant. At best, a unique issue. A trial copy, or a proof of some kind. It could be the book that Ward Lock intended to publish, mentioned in Beeton's Annual, but which has never been located.'

'How much?' enquired the always direct Mr Dryfeld.

'Ten to twenty. Grand. Plus.'

Jamie woke with a spastic jerk, spilling the dregs of his whisky over the pages, which Nicholas Lane mopped frantically with an indescribable handkerchief. He ran out, now, his last long-reserved line, and snorted, while Jamie gazed on, waiting, unsuccessfully, for the invitation to take a brotherly poke.

'Twenty grand, Up. Way up, if it comes to auction in New York.'

The febrile and inhumanly sharpened and quickened brain of Nicholas Lane had perfect recall of every catalogue, article, book he had ever had through his hands. "Nettley" was a spelling that didn't exist in any known version of the text. He had, once again, uncovered a piece of history, a true splinter of the 1880s. And this was it, this was the big one, the white whale, the reason why we're all in the game: he'd brought it in, finally, the ultimate score. And it was for sale.

Once Dryfeld had found the Department of Health and Social Security and shoved his anonymous document denouncing Mossy for child-abuse through the letterbox there was nothing else to do. They had burnt this place to the ground, there were other places to look for.

2

A WHARFINGER is a man of business, and eats accordingly. John Gull, Senior, his back to the land, attended to his breakfast with a severe and methodical concentration. He did not make two cuts where one cut would serve. Even the flesh of swine could be brought to use, divided in moral symmetry, tasted, swallowed, the worthy elements put to work, the worthless burnt in the stomach's pit, stamped down, expelled: the sheep parted from the goats.

His great head like a trophy, unmoving, eyes fixed on the panels of his door, as if waiting for the day's commandments to appear there; while, secretly, his hands served him, as his children did, his wife, his labourers. These hands, set off by starched cuffs, were honourably blackened, the nails broken; he was not too proud to exercise his talents, his pride was in the sweat of his brow.

His fist, like a pale crab, went among the warmed meats, slither of kidney, liver, blood-sausage, layered on thick muscular segments of potato. He chewed vigorously, exercising an already powerful jaw; animal fires became his fires. There was no pleasure of the senses in this. Work was life, life was work. *"Blessed is he who has found his work."* The weak must serve the strong, and be protected, as children served their parents, as women served men, as men served God: that savage and wonderful darkness.

His strong square teeth split the eye of an egg, squeezing the unfertilized life onto his tongue. He nodded assent as his wife,

Elizabeth, lifted the kettle from the hob and brought it to him for his final cup.

He drowned the well-mashed food with scalding fern-water tea.

Young William watched him. The child was silent as the man. His stillness remarkable, utterly contained, acknowledged by his father, who allowed him to remain, standing, his chin at the edge of the table.

John Gull smoothed the cord of his moleskin waistcoat over a full but obedient stomach. A man of business. And the creature of his God. Above him, on the wall, a wooden board had been hung, no mere decoration, the legend burnt into its varnished skin: **Whatsoever thy hand findeth to do do it with thy might.**

Black uneven marks. Runes. Sticks floating in gravy. The board balanced above John Gull's head like a conjurer's hat. These were shapes that could work miracles, could change the house into a boat. William saw his father above him, elbows upon the table, a man-tabernacle, his head in a helmet of letters.

The morning lightened, it was time to work. The sea was in the river and the river over the land. Rime and fret and rain, tides drifting in air, an unshaped world of ditch and channel. There were fish in the trees and owls swimming.

His house was an upturned boat. There were no others. We are the only people in the world, thought William. We are the first ones, the chosen. This is our Ark. The world is water. But we shall be sent out over all the great wide fields of the ocean: we shall look upon God's face. We are his Gull.

*

Aloga taimma a gaoow liifbb a baogy ho livin a hao s. The sharp point of the stone cut out a white trace against the slate. Sunlight flashed and darted on the estuary. William's fingers pushed the stone up and down, taking pleasure in gouging a track for the letters he knew, but could not read.

'T-t-taking a likeness, I suppose? T-t-this fine Armada of your f-f-father's. Very cred-it-able.'

The tall shadow across his work stopped William. There was more, but now he would not mark it. The man breathed on his neck, warm horsebreath, as he bent to make a show of examining the work.

'Making a testa met.'

The stranger sniffed at such precociousness and, without being invited, the child showing no sign of rising, sat on the ground alongside him.

'W-w-will you read t-t-to me from your t-testament?' He took great care to stress the missing letter.

'Alongtimeagolivedaboywholivedinahouse.' He had written no more. But could continue. Most of the slate had been filled, nobody had shown him how to do it: he could do it on his own. There were more slates to be found along the shore. Their edges were sharp, you could cut the heads from fish. You could split your tongue if you licked them.

'A long time ago lived a boy who lived in a house. And it was big.'

'And the boy's n-n-name?' said the stranger.

William turned to look at him. It was a hot pink man, a man with a naked face who had glass over his eyes, who wore a hat and carried a bag on his shoulder. Who smelled of too much soap.

'I live in a house,' said William.

'D-d-do you live in t-that house?' There was no other. A line of cottages, solitary, to a purpose, set in front of unworked fields. Landermere. Water around them, reeds, inlets. There was nowhere else.

'I can write. I can make a testament, like the Old.'

'I also l-l-like to write,' replied the man, 'should you care to hear what I have w-w-written t-t-this morning?'

'No,' William answered, simply: he had seen his father and his brothers coming down the track from the cottage, coming to the quayside, to their quay. A cart could be heard, the other side of the trees, wheels creaking, well-loaded. There would be work. Sacks to carry. Barges to stack. Ropes to catch and make fast. His father would sail upon the sea.

'I s-s-should l-l-like to talk w-w-with your father,' the parson said, slipping his bag onto his shoulder, reaching for William's hand, withdrawing, turning, nodding, and striding off along the shore-path towards the complacent and uncomplaining fauna, cloud life, water life, tree stumps that let themselves be observed, described, sketched. And made no charge. Save on his time. Of which he was fortunate enough to have an abundant supply.

'That man has stripes on his forest,' thought William, 'I cannot teach him if he will not listen.'

Under the water the sisters are hiding. They will not climb into the sky until the huntsman has passed. But when it is the time to hunt then they will be hunted.

3

UNDER the grass stain, the altar. I dreamed a new dream, meadows of fire. Walking through a wood that is superimposed along the present line of Brick Lane. The force of the river taking me down, pulling me beyond the human heats, running out of time into the previous, ahead; nerved to a candle-flame consciousness.

There are figures carved upon the rocks, huge faces cut into the red mud of the bank: in the undergrowth, thread-like forms of star ancestors. The light is brown, a sluice of blood. Daring to pass the warning in the stone.

The movement now is south.

The field opens at the river's source, a white stone chapel, travellers might pray, pilgrims pause, not itself a shrine, a cause: a cure. Warm light, from high slits, blades the floor. A white enclosure. The clouds are rolling in a seamless loop, darkly from some unshriven act. I fall to the ground.

"One unknown, yet well known."

I am on my knees, a penitent. I do not yet know what confession to make.

You allow yourself to become saturated with this solution of the past, involuntary, unwilled, until the place where you are has become another place; and then you can live it, and then it is.

*

Work takes us to strange places.

They examine my arms and legs for needle tracks. They whisper numbers. They hold up letters for me to recognise. I am taken on: my name is entered in the book.

The ullage cellar looks out on a broad and cobbled yard. We work under the sign of the Black Eagle, the plague year date, the number of the beast disguised in gothic script: to the sound of bells from the belltower, dividing the labours of the day.

As the carts draw into the yard we tumble out the eleven and twenty-two gallon barrels and kegs, shifting weights that might have seemed unmovable, by being expected to shift them. We are beyond ourselves, part of a team: the cellarman, the sculptor and I.

The kegs are then run on their rims, kicked and rolled, down the ramp into the cellar itself, out of the light, set into their lines. And here you run into risk. The caps that stand out from the keg-heads are unlocked so that the levels can be measured, the slops tested, the flat lager dipped, and one in four, or perhaps five, goes up, like a grenade, a great amusement to the cellarman with his clipboard and pencil, blasting the aluminium pipe high into the air, or the face of the novice tester.

After the third keg has been safely defused a pale reluctance comes over the operatives. Boot laces unravel, braces need adjusting, caps fall off. There is a shuffling and scratching, a lighting of cigarettes.

Up she goes! Better to shake her and force the issue, get it over. Then on into the darkest reaches of the cellar, splashing through ankle-high tides of unanalysed liquids, sharp animal movements, sensing the cracks and bung-holes.

The condemned returns are brought to an open pit and tipped away into a slate tank, into rumours of underground caverns, labyrinths, ancient cold-blood life forms: a stomach tightening rush of sourness. Measure of wheat for a penny and three measures of barley. Liquid voices.

What happens then is not our concern. The cellarman kicks out, savagely, splitting a rat's belly with his metal-capped boot; then the broom handle. Another kick drops the body in the sluice, old beer washes it away in a flood. You drink it.

The workers sweat and pull, get stuck in, move through fear, boredom, exhaustion for a good hour, clearing the task. And then the time is their own. Out to the drivers' bar where the beer is free. Heavy gutted men, shoulder to shoulder, tank up for the road. With sweeteners to come, days of drinking, over-time nights. To the hot food counter and a 24 hour breakfast.

I sat out in the doorway, mopping my neck with a handker-chief, taking the sun with old Dick Brandon, risking haemor-rhoids upon a black stone bollard. Dick tipped, from a tin jug, his first pint of porter; drank, thin neck convulsing. He could have my jug as well: on this base our relationship was founded.

I wanted to listen and absorb, he talked. He did not need any audience, or prompting. He didn't tell the stories, they told him. Stooped old man, veins bumping in transparent skin, the flawed smoothness of something left too long in water: voice from an uninhabited shell. Everything extraneous to the story had been eaten away, fed now only by the drink that he him-self brewed. Unnoticed; his words ignored by the other work-men, busy notching up the overtime, playing the angles, pol-ishing the hub cabs of their bile-coloured Rovers, carving out those little necessary extras.

'Used to watch fires (sniff): seen wards of the city go up like when they burn the stubble; seen clocks melt (sniff); seen horses on fire break out of them stables, down Woodseer cross Deal, up on the railway, *seen 'em*, manes flaming, run straight (bang) into a train. (Sniff) Seen fires starting when there wasn't not nobody to start 'em.

Nights all up in that tower room, windows blinded, looking out all across the roofs; not nobody on the streets, was there? Little drink, fag, like, if I wanted, go out on the parapets, I do; go where I like, walk, Flower and Dean, Thrawl, Heneage,

Chicksand, walk cross the river if I wanted, nobody else, not never touched the ground. Like a goat then, weren't I? Didn't 'ave no weight. Knew every bleeding stone on it and still do. Look there, that church, been all through it; like a bird, mate, nothing changed.

'Nother time, wasn't it (sniff)? I hear the siren, but I never shifts. Bethnal Green Station. Thousands, mate! Pouring your river into a piss bottle. On the stairs, a woman with a kid, she fell. And more of 'em, then, wouldn't hold back. Wall of bodies, all joined up, that's what they said. Breath sucked all out. Pushing in from behind. A hundred and seventy bleeding three. Dead. Closed it up, bury't 'em where they was.

Best morning, mate, best morning, armband, bicycle, Autumn it was, bit of mist, warm. Called out (sniff) to the Jews' Burial Ground, weren't I? Down Brady Street; never go before, never wanted. Great big bleeding wall up all round. Durward Street, cottages then, a bomb, they said, in the night, a whistle, two or three in the morning.

Made an old Jew feller let me in; wouldn't say nothing, would he? Little door in the wall, slow with 'is key, long pockets. Not nobody goes in there till the barber's 'ad 'is ring for 'is watchchain. Bottled walls. What's the matter, mate? I says to him, 'fraid they'll climb out?

All them graves faces one way, black, sod-ugly tongues, waiting on a sermon. Wheels the bike in, don't I? Quiet, he's got me at it; no birds in 'em trees, earth's dead, mud; wouldn't see a wasp in there. Not the same for those bastards, is it? Burnt stones, all black; was looking for the bleeding methos. Can't see no bomb neither. All mist, mate; trousers sopping, could 'ave pissed meself.

And then, I don't know, push my bike in an 'ole, not nearly. Urns all smashed, tipped on over, stones; got to report it, ain't I? 'Ave a blow, old mate, a light, just five. Blimey, the roof! Springfield Park? I'm telling you. Protocols of Zion, what! These Jews, Fathers, sitting on the roof of this little 'ouse, they've got, office, what you call it? Black 'ats down on their faces, beards. Looking, pointing. Not me, mate. Starting to laugh. Blimey! Ever seen 'em laugh? Day of bleeding Judgment. Bits of 'em all over that roof. Just bits. 'Anging to it, falling off of. Laughing! Never seen nothing like it nowhere. The men that will not be blamed for nothing. No, mate!'

*

As I cultivated Dick Brandon so the sculptor, S. L. Joblard, cultivated Mr Eves of the Publicity Department. Mr Eves had a collection of photographic plates taken, by long exposure, at the sites of the Jack the Ripper murders; all the courtyards, doorways, factory gates. Some of which he would show, some of which he would not. He was rumoured to have other things also.

There were so many unrecorded rooms hidden in the secret architecture of the brewery, chambers under the roof, passageways blocked by pipes, vaults beneath the cold store, condemned stables, locked cupboards. The old ones, Brandon and Eves, went where they wanted: unreachable and free to follow their own obsessions. So that afternoon would find Dick Brandon asleep in a hammock of his own contriving, slung between two warm pipes, a nest of wild cats beneath him; would find Mr Eves, hands in white cotton gloves, carding his collection or, cyclops-eyed, viewing his photographs through an ivory-handled magnifying glass, waiting for the first trace of movement somewhere among the grey background detail; would find Joblard and Sinclair out on the streets.

The zone was gradually defined, the labyrinth penetrated. It was given limits by the victims of the Ripper: the Roebuck and Brady Street to the East, Mitre Square to the West, the Minories to the South, the North largely unvisited. Circling and doubling back, seeing the same sites from different angles, ferns breaking the stones, horses tethered on wastelots, convolvulus swallowing the walls, shadowed by tall tenements, chickens' feet in damp cardboard boxes, entrails of radio sets, slogans on the railway bridge, decayed synagogues, the flash and flutter, cardamom seeding, of the coming bazaar culture, the first whispers of a new Messiah.

We wilfully lost the time, and ourselves: from the Nazrul, a surfeit of cockroaches, to the Seven Stars, by way of the Betting Shop. Trying the resilience of previously-unpunished digestions.

When two men meet a third is always present, a stranger to both.

4

IT HIT Dryfeld more slowly than it hit the narrator but the spikehead reacted with sharper despatch. Left his room, oilskin blinds drawn, strip-lighting dripping its sick and erratic pulse, radio jabbering World Service to a deserted floor of books, skulls, overcoats: took his bicycle from against the wall and went east.

This might be the morning when he found the second volume of Meyerstein's Chatterton biography and rounded off the suicide collection. If all the books were netted there would be no reason to hang about: he could top himself.

The Late Watson was lying in bed and the thought of twenty thousand pounds seemed suddenly like a workable slab of time; he realised, sweating, that a piece of it could be his. The agreement stood: Nicholas Lane took the 19th century fiction, he took the 20th, Dryfeld took everything else – *unless* anything turned up with a selling price of more than a grand; then they split it three ways. Jamie was out, couldn't handle the kind of arrangement that struck him as being tantamount to communism. He understood auctions. You just turned up. Didn't bid. Agreed to keep your hands in your pocket, with his problems, no great hardship. You picked up the divy.

A slice of twenty thou was out there: it didn't feel like his, unearned, and the chances of getting it unless he acted – NOW . . .

The warmth of his wife, asleep, moving against his side; he could hear Dryfeld's voice. 'Part-timers!' The ultimate insult.

Dryfeld padlocked his wheels, winding a heavily-guaranteed chain in and out of the spokes, round the crossbar, over the rail that fronted a strip of wasteground to the side of the Carpenters Arms; holdall extracted from the wooden box he'd had made to carry a few of his purchases; spun on his heel, no glimpse at the masonic symbols cut into the glass of the pub door, no thought for the owners, Ron and Reg, languishing in exile, without even a decent publisher for their verses.

Things were dead, just after midnight, and only the first two or three vans had pulled in to the Vallance Road end of Cheshire Street. Men in jackets like aircraft fitters stood around the vans doing their best to look as if these vehicles had nothing to do with them – until anyone moved in to take a look, when they suddenly reappeared, inside the tailboards, looking very much as if it was *everything* to do with them and that any citizen who disputed it would get a toecap up his adam's apple.

These were the legendary backs of lorries that things fell off of, John. Including torch-holders, with yard long torches, demonstrating their success with vicious cigars, their expertise by economy of language, all of it foul. Conversation is not a requirement, neither is a cheque book. American Excess cards can be bought by the fistful, but not used, except for forcing locks.

Books, naturally, do not feature high on the list of desiderata for this fraternity. They won't make a show until a couple of hours before first light, along with the pocket-torch dealers, with a poke no bigger than a couple of hundred, who are permanently scuffling around trying to borrow, or sell what they have already found, to buy-in the *real* stuff which has just surfaced, in rumour, on the next corner. The general junkmen don't buy books but are, grudgingly, prepared to take them for free. And start them at fifty. By the time the punters appear at half-eight they're down to a tenner. Take 'em away for a dollar by opening time.

Dryfeld growls through the vans, pokes into sacks, storms among the sheds of rag pickers, elbows over terminal wastelots, where old bones have been spread out to dry, more for exhibition than with any serious expectation of a sale. He snarls back at the caged animals, bird yelp, rancid fish tanks, heavy-jaw'd fighting beasts dealt, as they have been for over a hundred years, under the railway arches. The sentiment of the local inhabitants flattered by having some creature whose existence is even worse than their own. There is no sighting of Nicholas Lane. He's gone underground so deep he'll come up with mud on his nose.

The narrator locks his car in Palissy Street; wail of high pipe mountain music, with sewing machine percussion, from single lit window in the block of minatory tenements. They put up these dreadnought hulks to replace the dustheaps of the Nova Scotia rookery. Arnold Circus a-twitter with bird frenzy, the stones limed with droppings.

Stop off for onion rolls and croissants, then down the Lane, cut into the first left turn, wall painting faded, an historic quotation, *"I'm going home / to my / BACON STREET / radio"*; merest glance over a drain of paperbacks, records, amputee dolls, single shoes. It's too late, the Outpatients are already twitching into every crevice.

Seasonal plague. Spring surprises them: they emerge, pale, clutching their giros, rucksacks at the ready, to deal paper. They scavenge the scabby lots and burn down the charities. Buy at the bottom and polish the prices, always rubbing, scratching out the originals; cycle back to Camden Passage and Camden Lock with ever-growing bags, cases, sacks of half-respectable waste, the Penguin Classics: strictly for penguins. Who waddle up to the stalls with numbers to check in their notebooks. Books for bingo callers.

At high summer the mania speeds: the valium stash is running low. They shift to amphetamine mania. Bug-eyed, they shovel through the diseased end of Portobello Road on a Friday, competing with a triad of moon-faced Hong Kong hustlers, ready to deal anything, quantity is what they're after: the dealers at the bottom get more and more and more stock, meaning that they can't or won't sell it, while the dealers moving up have less and less, which gets progressively more expensive, until they've got nothing but a chair, a telephone, and a West Coast phone-number. Saturday, Bell Street, plus ten jumble sales, Fulham to Finchley, more and more territory, faster and faster, to find less and less, no time to look, grab anything, fill the bag, until you can hardly walk, dipped shoulder: by Thursday the stress has really begun to bite. They've been known to crack wide open, slap the face of some innocent walking down Essex Road to catch a bus to work. 'It's gone, it's gone! Oh Jesus, oh God! My *Waterland's* been stolen; oh no, oh Christ!' Sobbing on the floor, tearing fingernails in a shriek down the glass walls of Mr Carrier's Restaurant. Holiday's over, back to the funny farm.

The Outpatients, also referred to as Neck-Breathers, angry, puffed with thyroidal angst, love Brick Lane, but they're not to be confused with the Scufflers or the Stoke Newington austerity freaks, the glums. The Scufflers have their pretensions: have seen books change hands for money, have hoarded catalogues, from which they never order (not realising that the catalogued books are the ones that the big boys can't sell, sour stock). They want top dollar.

The Scufflers attach themselves, if they can, to radical charities. It's a great scam, collecting first editions for the Sandinistas, wheedling letters of support from John le Carré, town hall courtesy of Nuclear Free Islington: flog it all off, top wack.

The Scufflers mainly like to fight over tables. To hell with books. They've got to get the best pitch and the most tables. If something doesn't sell it's because the table isn't big enough. They'll kill for the longest stall.

They fan out through the market like a commando unit: booted, combat gear, hands like hooks, despising the old street-traders and loudly arguing over every price. The panic doesn't set in until they do actually find something; then comes the terror, they might have to *sell* it and GET THE PRICE WRONG! Better to bury or burn it.

They've come wholly into their own in the bleak days of enterprise zone capitalism, lame dogs, mad dogs, and the weak to the wall. All the floating street literature has been trawled-in and priced out of the range of any remaining students who might like to sample it. A cultural condom has been neatly slipped over the active, the errant and beautiful tide of rubbish.

Dryfeld and the Late Watson spot Nicholas Lane at the same moment, converge, each grabbing a bone elbow. They're lucky to find him. He's altogether too good a dealer for what this place has become. The generations of street dealers, like mayflies, can pass in weeks, days; a trip out of town, it's gone, and it never comes back. When the Scufflers have found it, Nicholas Lane is no longer there. If you hear his name – it's too late.

One last nostalgic circuit; he's not even buying books, his amazing radar has homed on a photograph of T. S. Eliot presenting a Wyndham Lewis portrait to some Canadian academics who look as if they've fallen off a totem pole. It's inscribed, of course. If Nicholas Lane is around, there's something worth finding. He's an alchemist, turning shit to gold, and gold straight back to shit again.

We can hear the Scufflers beating down some tattered Colin Wilsons from 20p to 5p: unsuccessfully. Overpriced at nothing.

*

The coffee in the grease caff is very slightly preferable to the tea: it hits like a hammer, a mild concussion, instead of permanent kidney damage. The dead egg slides off a damp white sheet of bread.

Nicholas Lane's emaciation is extraordinary and active, like a cancer inherited from a centuries old act, now flowering. Some dead man's crime shines in his face. He is high on enthusiasm, pinched with cold, shivering in his black, wild with speculations and futures. *A Study in Scarlet* was yesterday and the word is, ON.

The word with Dryfeld is *murder*. And now is too late. He wants a sale and he wants a share. The creditors of his creditors have grown old waiting, the machete blades are blunt that once had the ambition of kneecapping him, but the cry of neglected treasures in remote provincial bookshops is too piercing and insistent. He wants to get there: in a first-class compartment.

He's coming to Lane's place that night and he wants his money. Before his coffee cup shatters on the table the entire caff, who have been forcibly listening to him roar, can turn and see him cycle past the window, up West, to watch a daylong Abel Gance film, on three screens. Energy is also a form of possession.

Nicholas bags the Eliot snap, no craziness to sell, no desperation to hold. 'I'm sure of one thing. It's the end now. The cycle's over. Nothing more. The end of the world. That's definite. You can actually *see* the millennial tremble, man.'

Thin, stained, fingers dipping and twitching over the sugar bowl; fingers like a fist of noses, shredded fine on the strings of an acoustic guitar, ichorate ghost of a rock musician. Remember that this man was on the bill with Bob Dylan at the Isle of Wight; was shortlisted to replace Brian Jones. It wasn't his finger skills that blacked him, but the power of his nostrils. Their pepper ration was threatened.

He tilts the table with sudden fears. The colour runs out of his eyes. It's true but you can't see it. The end now. All over. Running into ourselves, running.

Old hippie, old monk. Nicholas Lane rises, to shake hands, an exquisite and natural courtesy; and leaves, through the crowd, faint shadow.

*

You can be so much in a room that the world outside turns to water. You've got the heater blowing out burnt air but you still don't get warm. Your ankles are singed but your head's in a bucket of ice. Time drips like a stalactite. The water for the coffee boils away in a tree of steam.

Young Kernan was a rock goffer, wounds running back to the prehistory of the early 70ies, a maimed generation, like survivors of the first war, smiling, divine lit, never the same again, damaged, twitchy but blessed with the face of a recently roger'd altarboy. He'd followed Nicholas Lane through the great times into the bad, the worse, the bottom of the pit, looking somehow as if he was just back from a birching at the sauna. His clothes were in rags but he still had it, the newborn optimism of a true disciple who couldn't believe it was all over. Someone should have slapped a preservation order on him. But in the new world of deals there is no contact sex.

He poured, from a blackened pan, hot water onto yesterday's grains. Small domestic epiphanies light the squalor. Postcards, tribal carvings, dead-dada, some children's toys. Old stories, not yet evaporated. Carpet worn to the boards. Set of scales. It's weigh-out time. Not top shelf shit, but it should cut seven ways. Six to sell and one to keep. Pay out £650 to make £50. It takes a lot of work to keep work at arm's length, to carry on working.

The Late Watson waited, what else. There was no point in trying for any other business. The mirror, the razor, the scales. Just pick up a book and read.

Somewhere, *A Study in Scarlet*: in his cabinet, that briefcase, or stashed? There's a lot of night still unused.

In the street outside D/S Clark and Policewoman Dudley, on watch, revolve between the pub, which is the busiest brothel between Cable Street and Whitechapel, black guy running white women, disgusting, and the half-squat, a warren of garment outworkers, raincoat button-holers, kite dyers: all of them dealing. Where to start? Nothing worth kicking back.

'See that Hessel Street. Worse than Calcutta. They're butchering on the bloody pavements. Living in caves, the animals.'

And while he lays out his experience of local colour he makes a trial of his hand upon his subordinate's black stocking'd thigh, fiercely muscled, meeting no resistance.

The staked heart of John Williams, the Ratcliff Highway Murderer, beats evenly at the quadrivium, at peace, from the shuntings of the work ethic, connected in a mysterious and unspoken thread to the recently scoured white stone blocks of St George in the East.

5

JOHN GULL got his living from the water, shifting the fruits of the fields, by barge, from Hamford Water to the City of London, measures of wheat, measures of barley; and, in London, he got his death from water. It was always there and always with him. The comma-bacillus had not yet been named; unchristened, it was deadly.

The communal water-pump at Broad Street had been infected, sewage and water running together, harsh summer, the strings hanging from the boxes in Spitalfields Market were black with flies; Gull's vegetables rotting in heaps; ants ran to the very steps of the church in such numbers that they could be taken up a handful at a time; the mad croaking of frogs.

The sun became black as sackcloth of hair, and the moon became as blood.

Gull's blood boiled: and turned to water. His willed boundaries burst, he flooded into nothingness. Grit on the facade of lion-crusted buildings. Dust on the optimism.

Elizabeth, his wife, who had taken no firm stand on anything while John Gull lived, now that he was dead, insisted, was not to be shaken from the strangest, some said paganistic, cannibal island, demand. Grief had turned her, they said. But there was no outward show of grief. She was not what she had been. The bargemen, from respect, from a darker fear of John, that it should still be his voice speaking, obeyed her.

So it was that the longest, the blackest, the heaviest, the most imperial of John Gull's barges came back to Landermere. The cholera victim, swaddled in white, bound close, unforgiving: his heat sealed. Came round the Naze and down Hamford Water, along Horsey, along Skipper's Island; the birds of the estuary wheeling, a dull flat beaten-sun morning, early, the skin of water feverish, flinching from harm, breezeshifting: a straggle of neighbours, obedient, subdued, Elizabeth and William, the boy, at the quay.

The bargemen, bareheaded, gave way; Elizabeth herself then leading the great horse, the Suffolk Punch, that dragged John Gull in his oversize floating coffin through close channels and cuts, among reeds; William following, a muzzled wolf.

They curved from sight of the line of solitary cottages. The bargemen, their wives, remaining, eyes on the imageless water, turned away: so many turnips on sticks.

In a place that was neither land nor water, in a field that had been cast adrift, unworked, the horse was freed from his harness. And the barge was fired.

John Gull's back was to the sea when his bones broke from his flesh. His skull, lying in only inches of water, burst into flame, a lantern. He seemed to rise, to sit; bent, like a dry branch. His bird, a shard of black cloth, lifted, blazed, was gone.

The woman and the boy stood through the long afternoon. That place was theirs: unknown, it was shunned.

William Withey Gull, his red eyes brilliant in a blackened face, his cropped hair ashed into age, an old man, screamed out over the reeds in savage laughter.

*

The parson's ambition would never now be satisfied in full: he could talk to William's father, but would get no reply. He could talk as well to a fence-post or to one of the stones marking the channel across the mud to Horsey Island. He *had* talked to them; incontinent, solitary of speech, uncontradicted, he ranted at crows, he flattered the hedges, he debated with maggots in a rabbit's skull, he checked improprieties among the flints. Men of the cloth live in this monologue, it is their due: nobody talks back to a pulpit.

John Gull's defiant silence quickened, sharpened, enlarged his desire to open a conversation with his relict, Elizabeth.

The widow was a woman of moderate height, dark, full-figured. She smoothed her hair, but made no other gesture to vanity, before opening her door to the scratching of Mr Harrison, Rector of Beaumont.

Mr Harrison lived with the sand running through his fingers, the grains gushing from his spine, time was his fear: gone, gone, gone. Night sweats. The yawning grave. For ever. Clay on his eyes.

Each morning he felt the bones of his face, probed for a weakness, a sagging of the skin. He needed to be about, to be moving, doing: man of air and fire, fierce, high conceits. He plucked and tore at the vine around the cottage doorway; stooped, twisted his thin neck, as if to peer through the cracks in the wood.

'Ah, M-M-Madame, M-Mrs Gull, I . . . Dear L-Lady, umm . . .'

William Gull had preceded his mother and now his head, a solid one, came into contact with Mr Harrison's nervously tensed and contracted stomach.

'Y-Yes . . . I . . . M-Madame . . .'

The widow's hair was backlit, he stumbled among correspondences drawn from the masters of The School of Venice. Her hand, on William's shoulder, was strong, not delicate, a plain gold band married to her finger.

'Sir?'

'If I m-might . . .?' Mr Harrison stepped back, gesturing wildly; William following him out and countering his intention of coming forward once more towards the door.

'Would you care to come into my house, sir?'

He would, he did: manoeuvred, standing, falling, half-bowing, colouring, gesturing, starting up, staggering, uninvited, to a seat at the fireside.

"Whatsoever thy hand findeth to do . . ."

What Mr Harrison wished to do, he could not; what Mr Harrison might, in good christian conscience, do – he did. William Gull should attend at Beaumont Rectory each evening, on his return from the village school, and would be tutored, in the Classics, in the revealed word of our Lord, in the observation and description of flora and fauna, both local and general, in the peregrinations of heavenly bodies. There might even be the opportunity, under the closest supervision, of course, of sampling the choicest effusions of the finest poets of the day, such as Sir Walter Scott.

This was satisfactory to Mrs Gull, it was satisfactory to Mr Harrison, and would, in the fullness of time, the rector was confident, be quite satisfactory to Mr Benjamin Harrison, an uncle, who was the Treasurer, no less, of Guy's Hospital, Southwark, London. The hospital already being William's landlord, would, in the person of Mr Benjamin Harrison, God willing, William fulfilling his evident, and inherited, promise, and working with all his given abilities, also be his patron. A path was open, winding from the waterside, circuitously, to Beaumont, through many trials and dangers, both moral and physical, many tests of will, to the great world. He should . . . serve.

Mr Harrison allowed himself, with this torrent of benevolence, to clamp Mrs Gull's hand between two of his own. To draw her hand up a little way towards his lips, then drop it, so that it fell, palm upwards, on the table: a dead white fern, prophetically engraved, creased with the awful future.

6

MR EVES had the victims' names printed in red on brittle vinegar-coloured cards, black bordered. The first letter of each name had been capitalised and enlarged, illuminated in a densely ornamented block. He took the cards out of a shoebox and held them against his chest, uncertain what to bid.

Joblard and Sinclair leant back from the table, eager, respectful of Eves' time; feigning a calm they did not feel. Sharing a jug of porter, heavy headed, slopped into china mugs. Eves waved aside their offer.

'Diabetic. Won't see New Year. Bugger the injections. Go when I'm ready and go in my own way. Won't play the yogi, no.'

His skin was waxy and fibrous, unset parchment, cheeks hollow; refined by disease, eaten away to a great delicacy of gesture and movement. Skipping on inessentials.

Dealt out the name cards, a kind of tarot, across the green baize table. His cork-like head nodding across the panes of the small leaded windows. Dark wood behind him. Afternoon tutorial in an Oxford College. The world at a distance.

Mary Ann Nichols, Annie Chapman, Elizabeth Stride, Catherine Eddowes, Marie Jeanette Kelly.

'No more.' He anticipated us. 'Your Tabrams, your Myletts, not part of this. The chapel could have swallowed them at any time. They wobbled over. Not willed. But look at my names – what do you see?'

We saw names, we knew the names. There were other versions

of them, the victims might have rendered themselves in a dozen ways, so did Shakespeare – did they remember who they were? These were the names of the victims and they were locked together like a famous football team: they were inseparable. Part of the doctrine.

We stared at the cards. Mr Eves turned from us, reaching for a thermos of tea, poured it, unsteaming, cooled, elbow-dipping temperature, ladled in a few inches of sugar, cup of old dandruff, stirred, sucked rather than drunk; pushed his white lips into the film-surfaced liquid. A smile, stumps of teeth, broken pencils, rabbit mouthed. He had successfully posed a riddle: we had to solve it. He was going nowhere. Retired, for ever, to his scriptorium. The work was done.

'Take 'em,' he said, tapping the cards with an uncut fingernail, 'they don't mean anything to me anymore.'

He swivelled a desktop magnifying glass, put his thumb against it, a tongue in a window. The whorl forensically enlarged.

'This is the true spiral,' he said, 'the first map of the labyrinth.'

*

> But most through wintry streets I hear
> How the midnight harlot's curse
> Blasts the new born infant's tear
> And smites with plague the marriage hearse . . .

Drumming Blake, Blake drumming like a madness, one of those sugar-hook addictions that get into your head, a spasm, won't be shifted: set against local pain, pulsing against bodily exhaustion.

The sign of the Pleiades hangs, stars joined into a pint pot, over a public house on the west side of Brick Lane: The Seven Stars. Brides of the Pleiades. 'Brides' being the familiar name in this quarter for whores. Star-brides, servants of Orion. Lit corruptions. Do what you will shall be all of the law.

We settle in an oblique corner, bar still empty, sun puddle;

the stripper not due on stage for another thirty minutes. Joblard rolls a smoke between large, acid-stained, fingers. A changeling, his face unset. Young man with ash in his hair; mask of power submerged in pleasantries. Performs himself with such practised application that this presented self is become a true self: beneath it a larger mystery. He appeared full-grown, with no luggage, and a palaeolithic past. Marking the bone: nervous of paper.

The wall behind us repeats a scene of disembarkation; masts, castles, dancing. And suddenly I recognise the sentence that Eves has given us.

Mary Ann Nichols, Annie Chapman, Elizabeth Stride, Catherine Eddowes, Marie Jeanette Kelly. MANACESCEMJK. MANAC. ES. CEM. JK. MANAC ES CEM, JK.

The cold truth of that fiction is between us. Inrush of Sumerian breath. The bar, without transition, is filled: men coming in from the brewery, already half-cut, to jape and patronise the Sikh publican, cramming a wall, shoulder to shoulder, from street-door to Gents, enclosing the half stage in fetid attention.

Joblard takes from his jacket pocket a paperback account of the Moors Murders. Flicks through the text, inscribing, on a beermat, the names of the victims; *John Kilbride, Lesley Ann Downey, Edward Evans.* Arriving at the dreadful statement: JK, LADEE.

Wall of glass, a board stage. None of it matters. There is her time and our time. There are the workers, who have always been workers. For them it is time out. Manac. *"What doth the Lord require?"*

The girl is not, like many who work this pitch, deformed. She is notable in the clear skin of her self-knowledge. A black gauze shirt; sitting, ignoring the pens of hot faced draymen, plumbers, cutters, steaming, shirts soaked at the armpits, held back to the occasional bellowed obscenity.

She starts with her back to them, herself in the long mirror, a film, the shadow of herself; unconnected, slowly stripping away everything, revealing nothing, Inanna through the seven gates of Ereshkigal's Temple. They fasten upon her their eyes of death, she hangs against the stalks of their desire. The ritual sours and dries.

She walks, naked, among them, high heel'd, dirty scarlet shoes, spangled with dull sequin stars, leper shoes, collects her tithe, smoking, clink of coins in a pewter pot.

They are on the street and the heat of the old story begins to work with them. The Nazrul again, gobbling spiced meats, saffron rice, mummia. Coupled men lazy at tables, sweet sweet cakes, condensed milk-sick pastries. A single white girl, painted like a fairground horse, nostrils flaring, outlined in scarlet varnish, dead confectionery eyes, sitting on the table edge. The men fondle and ignore her. She creaks back out to the street, leather skirt, gladiator.

A voice from the table behind them, 'Well, you made a killing,' from an empty booth; their nerves heightened, overtuned, dictating messages. 'You made a killing.'

Rain spores die on the paving stones, remote energies drawn down into the entropy of the spiral; vegetable forces, pallid ferns pushing the cobbled bricks apart.

We share a bottle of menstrual wine, vagrants; we spit into wild gardens. We lick cigar stumps. We kick walls.

The dwellings on the south side of the Jewish Burial Ground have been evacuated by keyholders, occupied by derelicts and vermin; doomed, the whole zone is doomed; the stones will be razed, brick from brick, their histories flattened, buried in dust mounds. The geology of time is available to us now, at this moment, this afternoon, and will be gone, will be forever unreachable. Unredeemed.

Steps lead up to an openair chapel; high crenellated wall, arched, roofed, summer house, place of worship. Like a dockside; three triangle peaks painted with the eye of Horus. A half savage Baptist garden; tenement ravines all around, keeping out the light; shadow garden, balconies, stairwells, dark entrances. There are twin tablets set into the wall, tract commandments, for eyes lifting from the drone of psalms.

On the right: "Labour/ is life/ blessed is he/ who has found/ his work." The work that was short was life. Soon finished. Crushed.

On the left: "Whatsoever/ thy hand/ findeth to do/ do it with/ thy might."

Sixteen windows to the block, and four more set into the roof: blind eyes. Condemned time. This pre-rubble set, held upright on beams. The enduring strength of slums. Bearded charities built to last for a thousand years.

Five arches to the altar shed, the umbral body of the chapel; unattended god trap.

We made shift to the Brewery, let the trace in the ground lead us, the hare foot. A tide pulls us around islands of dereliction, gypsy spaces, remnants of civic concern, carefully plaqued, railway arches worked with wrecked motors, scrap melt. Through Durward to Vallance, cut down Buxton Street towards the back gate of the Brewery, to punch out.

A group of mid-Victorian cottages, marked for demolition, have been sealed with a corrugated iron fence. There is a poster, "SS", Nazi pastiche, radical, protesting Social Insecurity. As we read, a thin vermouth'd voice accosts us; glass tearing silk.

A woman with sauce-bottle hair, dyed rope, interprets for a small, wet skulled, shaking, tremulous, doll-like figure in pyjama trousers and carpet slippers. His armchair has been dragged out onto the pavement, out from where? Perhaps he lives in it. A few streaks of hair have been painted on his scalp, brown-red stain running down his pinched cheeks, like a hammer wound.

The woman has been told to ask if we are Germans.

Joblard, humoured with drink and exercise, raps out a few phrases of cod Mabuse. The little man contorts with real horror, kicking back his feet, dragging the great chair with him, covering his face with a thin arm.

The woman explains that he was in the camps; his name is Hymie, a tailor. They're going to pull down his house.

My wife and daughter have gone to stay for a few days with her mother, convalescing, within sight of the North Sea. Joblard returns with me, therefore, to run the afternoon into the night.

We tip out the fridge and eat it, shelf by shelf: olives, salad, rice pudding, bacon, cheese. Methodically swilling it down with a mix of Russian Stout and dry blackthorn cider. There remains only a chocolate cake of doubtful provenance, gifted by Divine Lit neighbours, by way of an Alice B. Toklas cookbook; and probably enlivened with middle-eastern additives.

Gorge, swill and choke; mouths black as mud gobblers. A good exhaustion and a buff envelope of bank notes in the pocket.

The cake has no immediate effect, we cram in a few more slices. And the television starts to acquire a previously unnoticed wit. Everything is ironic. Every remark is hilarious, but understated: nobody else could see it. We are lying on the floor, taking everything that is thrown at us, uncritical, amused. It's all the same, isn't it? Watch anything and find a value.

The programme we have been waiting for slides up on us, out of nowhere. The final shot in a television investigation of the Whitechapel Murders, *The Ripper File*.

In our deranged state there is no interest in following detail or making logical connections; we know it all. We shut our eyes: Masons, Clarence, Druitt, conspiracy, asylum. All that matters is the simple basic metaphor: three men, Sickert the painter, Netley the coachman, Gull the doctor. If the equation is neatly made, then it is true. The hair starts to rise on the scalp, there is some sort of recognition, names known, places known. It is confirmed merely.

We force ourselves to concentrate on the remote and ridiculous voices.

'*Do you have a picture of him?*'

'*Who?*'

'*Sir William Gull.*'

'*He looks a lot more important than the other two suspects.*'

'*He was. A self made man. Cured the Prince of Wales of typhoid and never looked back. He left £340,000 – a big fortune in those days.*'

'*Not bad now. Can you really see a man like that going down to Whitechapel and playing his part in the murder of five prostitutes?*'

I'm crawling towards the set, I'm forcing my face to look at it. Behind the wavering lines is a face that is firmer and better known to me than my own. It is the face of Joblard, the orphan.

Sir William Gull has stolen the orphan's face. His arrogance and self-containment chill me.

Does Joblard look at himself? Confront the self that is now accusing him, that knows him, that is pushing him to make himself available for the enactment of an ancient crime? The self that he has been unconsciously playing.

He does not: he's lying, face in the bathtub, groaning, watching the swill of regurgitated chocolate, curry, stout, *feathering*, clockwise, around the eye of the plughole.

The exchange of wills is postponed.

7

IT WAS THE FIRST TIME I had seen anybody cook with yogurt. Dark varnish, tall ceiling, window smeared with grease from steaming meats, oak and oilskin, the hull of the room bellying out over a small garden sprinkled with a scattered eruption of sickly plants: sleeves rolled neatly to the elbow, his large hands moved with forensic exactitude, scapula under the sizzling "black ornaments", *just* before they burnt, shook the rice in a separate pan, merely dipping the fingers of the green vegetables in boiling water. Old India hand.

The day was warm, expansive, blankets of yellow hammer-head flowers breaking out in a screech among the condemned gardens, the fenced lots. The long inertia was torn, the room-locked stiff-spined creaking winter people were irritated, ready to be moving, to get early among the streets; to search for it, find it, take it on.

But Joblard's heavy odd-paned windows were immovably fixed in ancient paint; a small coal fire red in the grate. He motioned me to his best armchair; we ate.

A surgery of tiny bottles, instruments, tubes, wires; a museum of stones, pelts, stuffed animals, hunters neutralised and grinning with the falsest of teeth; brass candlesticks; sepulchral clocks. So much of the past had been brought into these rooms that the air was smog and bistre; bone dust powdering his scalp, beard shadows set about our faces.

The hand twitched at the muffin bell to summon Mrs Hudson. Who seemed, in fact, to be present – for as the fire died the door would open and a stooping possessed man, affable but unfocused, would appear with a fresh coalbucket. The ash from a cigarhead detached – but before it reached the carpet it was swept into a pan by a diminutive, smiling, utterly sudden woman; so discreet that she was gone, clicking, before we had acknowledged her. The couple were like long resident poltergeists: we had strayed onto their territory and were to be served, unquestioned, but with no superfluous homage, no trace of irony.

There may have been other inhabitants, the house was tall, long windowed, calm – but they were not to be seen. Once some kind of animal manifested, a heap of old black fur, nodding-headed, half blind; slid a few feet towards the fire before being hurtled backwards and out on an invisible leash, the little woman clucking in the doorway.

From the front window: a few trees, a grass patch, sour clay and gravel, and beyond that, distant warrens of dark brick, unlit: under sentence.

Not having a violin or seven per cent solution within reach Joblard offered a clay pipe, himself sucking and digging at something more theatrical, shag soaked in rum. Time was brown with us, simmering, juicy. Smoke twisted into questions. Blue grey lights ran veins into the ceiling.

'I think,' said Joblard, indicating with his pipestem a copy of Stephen Knight's book, *Jack the Ripper, The Final Solution*, 'that we have been saved a great deal of donkey work. This scenario is remorselessly argued and, since it arrives at the cast-list we have already floated, we can accept it as a workable hypothesis and go on from there.'

'On?' I asked, 'or back?'

'There's something inherently seedy and salacious in continually picking the scabs off these crimes, peering at mutilated bodies, listing the undergarments, trekking over the tainted ground in quest of some long-delayed occult frisson. I abhor these hacks with their carrier bags of old cuttings.

If Mr Knight had been a chemist not a journalist I wonder if he would have chosen to describe any solution as "final". A solution, according to my dictionary, is "the act of separating the parts, specially the connected parts of any body." Unfortunate that. "The dissolving of a solid in a fluid; release; deliverance."

This is precisely what Knight's explanation does not procure. We are informed, heated, drawn into a collaboration with his version of the truth. But released and delivered? I think not. I don't think he understands that any delivery is required.

Or what monster might result from that bloody-handed parturition?

We acknowledge that there were five prostitutes killed by, or under the instruction of, Sir William Gull. A coach was involved, and a coachman, John Netley. The third man remains vaporous and loose faced. The events took place between August and November, 1888, in a specific location, Whitechapel.'

He paused, 'I like the idea of the grapes, too.'

He took up a limestone pebble from the table and twisted it nervously in his hand.

'Was this any more than a local conspiracy? Or is the cycle even now turning on us? As the century dies will another pattern of sacrifice be demanded? Do we slowly begin to understand only because we are about to become performers in the same blind ritual?'

Our conversation progressed in spasms and random leaps: dead frogs on an electric shelf. "From one drop of water," wrote Holmes in his article, *The Book of Life*, "a logician could infer the possibility of an Atlantic." But we were not logicians. We darted, snapped, disbelieved ourselves, turned back: always using the evidence of the past as our justification.

'I found something curious in Michael Harrison,' I began, 'published three years before Knight. Harrison claims, "What Sir William Gull had become to the Royal Family, Nobility and Aristocracy of Great Britain, in the field of medicine . . . Sherlock Holmes – even by the mid-'Eighties was well on the way to becoming in the field of protecting the Great from their enemies' malice . . ."

I think this is a better entry: by way of the shape that is unconsciously written into the text. What matters is what they don't say; but what is coded there, all that wonderful unexplained detail, like a Gothic Cathedral. That is how these books ensnare us in an addictive grip.

Peel down *Study in Scarlet* or *Jekyll and Hyde* or *Mystery of a Hansom Cab* and out come the prophetic versions. Beneath the narrative drive is a plan of energy that can, with the right key, be consulted.'

I took a copy of *The Sherlock Holmes Long Stories* out of my bag and prodded it over towards him. I had treated the text, like a prison censor, carefully blacking out, to uncover the mantic tremble beneath.

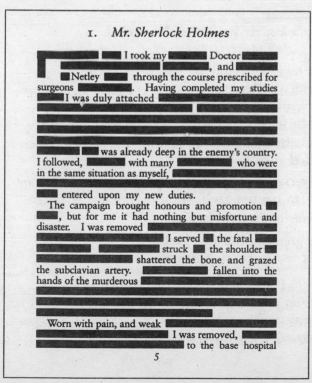

1. *Mr. Sherlock Holmes*

████████ ████ I took my ██████ Doctor ████████
███████████████████, and ████████
████Netley ██████ through the course prescribed for
surgeons ████████. Having completed my studies
████I was duly attached ███████████████████
██
██
██
████████ was already deep in the enemy's country.
I followed, ████████ with many ████████ who were
in the same situation as myself, ████████████████
████ entered upon my new duties.
The campaign brought honours and promotion ██
██, but for me it had nothing but misfortune and
disaster. I was removed ██████████████████
██████████ I served ██ the fatal ██████
██████████ struck ██ the shoulder ██
██████████ shattered the bone and grazed
the subclavian artery. ████████ fallen into the
hands of the murderous ████████████████
██
Worn with pain, and weak ████████████████
████████ I was removed,
████████████████ to the base hospital

'Obviously this is too blatant a reading. Better to take the flash of single words, cut phrases; let it build its own chain.'

"Netley. Surgeon. Horse.

London, that great cesspool.

Together in a hansom. Poor devil. Looking for lodgings.
Strange thing.
The second man to-day.

Couldn't get someone to go halves in some nice rooms.

Perhaps you would not care for him as a constant companion.
A little queer in his ideas.
Well up in anatomy.
Has amassed a lot of out-of-the-way knowledge.

Not a man that it is easy to draw out.
Avoids the place.

Some reason for washing your hands of the matter.

Cold-bloodedness.
A little pinch of the latest vegetable alkaloid.
May be pushed to excess.

When it comes to beating the subjects in the dissecting-rooms with a stick.
Rather bizarre shape.
Verify how far bruises may be produced after death.

Saw him at it with my own eyes.
Not a medical student?

Turned down a narrow lane and passed through
a small side-door which opened
into a wing of the great hospital.

Familiar ground. Needed no guiding.
No doubt you see the significance?

Let us have some fresh blood, he said.

Transparent fluid. Dull mahogany colour.
A brownish dust.
The stains are a few hours old.

Hundreds of men now walking the earth who would
long ago have paid the penalty of their crimes.

A man is suspected of a crime
months perhaps after it has been committed.
His linen examined.
Rust stains, or fruit stains?

Then there was Mason. The notorious.

I have to be careful. I dabble.

Discoloured with strong acids.
Know the worst of one another before they begin.

A mystery is it?

Much obliged to you for bringing us together."

'Dictation at this speed takes the scribe, often under pressure of work or disease, so fast and so deep that he writes it before it happens, and by writing it he causes it to happen, a fate game that allows the unconscious no release. He cannot escape his devils by describing them. The medium does not choose who he will serve.

This is to reverse the conventions of detective fiction, where a given crime is unravelled, piece by piece, until a murderer is denounced whose act is the starting point of the narration. Our narrative starts everywhere. We want to assemble all the incomplete movements, like cubists, until the point is reached where the crime can commit itself.

That is why there are so many Ripper candidates, so many theories: and they can *all* be right. They can all fade away in private asylums.

The Whitechapel deeds cauterized the millennial fears, cancelled the promise of revelation.'

We needed air: we would walk down to Southwark and examine the surgical tower.

*

Cobourg Road is a rib from a much older track, the pilgrim way, Old Kent Road, a turn beyond the Becket. This was an area that knew itself, valued itself; but lived with a fear of what was coming, and coming for them. Its secret could be violated: they were existing in suspended time and kept their voices low, made no demands.

Conan Doyle set many of his Sherlockian tales here. In this territory Dr Watson found a wife. The victims of crime awaited its visitation, not yet invaded by the angels of damage; mainline razors, nerve-clipt hatchetheads.

The zone was defended by its rigorous domesticity. The family remained a unit of force within its own walls, related and connected to so many other tribal alignments, van driving uncles, factory workers from the railway caverns: much could be shared, arranged, adjusted, small wrongs seen to. A closeness that was charmed; ordered, ritualised, unspoken. Social workers would unpick it, harm it with care, until it was gone forever.

When the underclothes of the first victim of the Ripper, Mary Ann Nichols, were examined they were found to bear the mark of the Lambeth Workhouse, which led to her identification as the wife of William Nichols, a printer, of Cobourg Road, Camberwell, from whom she had been separated for about nine years. The protection of this enclosure, not being visible or articulated, was erased in gin, burnt out, herself whored, cut loose, sucked inevitably, hauled in, from what she had played at being, down, mindless generosity, servant to Thrawl Street, Fournier, Flower & Dean, another more savage enclosure, the heated intestine of the city: she was slit, drawn out, unmeasured.

We break from this, carelessly. The Surrey Canal has dried; the old cholera line, work ditch, that did for John Gull. The unmarked passage out, to Greenland Dock and the Limehouse Reach, is a track of rubbish, waste, old streets tipped-in to dull its meaning. Maps of futility brought to ground.

There's nowhere to drink here: the pubs collapsed into their own pretensions, understudy villains ordering up cocktail froth, the mind-destroying jingle of electronic pickpockets.

Southwark holds its time, with the City, with Whitechapel, with Clerkenwell, holds the memory of what it was: it is possible to walk back into the previous, as an event, still true to this moment. The Marshalsea trace, the narrative mazetrap that Dickens set, takes over, the figures of fiction outliving the ghostly impulses that started them. The past is a fiction that absorbs us. It needs no passport, turn the corner and it is with you. The things they do there are natural, you do those things. Detached from this shadow you are nothing, there is nothing. You have no other existence.

Young doctors, with the yelping loudness of Bob Sawyer and Ben Allen, with that exuberance whose post-textual charm does not translate onto the street, shove into The Bunch of Grapes, to drink themselves steady for an afternoon in the cutting-rooms.

We cross St Thomas Street to reach the Red Tower.

A History of Pain under the protection of the cathedral rose: a threading of fruits, cornucopic horns, standing off the subdued brick. We enter, pay our coins, climb.

Under the eaves, the Herb Garret: here are the relics, the Whitechapel bell mortars, where friable bodies are reduced to powder. Here are the names of the Foul Wards; Lazarus, Job, Naples, Magdalen. Here is the warning: "The interest of the poor/ and their duty/ are the same." Under low rafters, the seed heads of poppies.

In the preserved operating theatre the light is septic, wound squeezed. The power of pain is honoured: with shavings, hacksaw, table, straps. The solidity of the cutting bench set against the curvature of the ochre galleries, as in Joblard's room. Above the head of the absent victim a tract is set: "Miseratione non mercede", to face the audience, the distinguished visitors on their padded chairs.

The floor has been raised three inches on joists to soak up the blood loss.

A paschal lamp hangs, blackened with the concentration of amputees, consciousness screaming with shock, forcing themselves to climb out from the pain, into the tracery of metal, into the light itself.

Long coated surgeons hack and cut, talking their virtuosity into the dry throats of the banked students. Splash the hands with water. A small looking-glass. Their own faces. Beards and teeth. The patients carried out. Performance concluded. The curtain of eyes.

Young Keats, lips bitten, attending. Neophyte. "Implicated" by these rituals in mysteries that made his heart too small to hold its blood. A torrent, that was not to be spoken, speeded by disease: witness.

Pus-spattered high boots, sour veins opened. Men of Guy's. Gull and Hinton; their private and secure theatre of gesture. Alchemy starts in the entrails of fear: birth-light in dung.

Escape. Heads tip forward, shoulders bruise on the church border: down Cathedral Street, a segmentary glimpse of tower and overhead railway in fractured combination, an expressionist film-set. Pick our way among grape boxes, under the roof-tree of the Borough vegetable market. Choose your entry.

If you can find a working market you'll find a pub worth drinking in. When the workers are gone – a quiet one.

We approach the Wheatsheaf, "TAKE COURAGE", wheels rattle across the top of the market, a maze of cages; packed carriages run out from the dome of St Paul's, shuddering.

The bar has its own sense of what it should be: damp wood bowed like whalebone, cabin-close, engravings of the old city, its secret corners, obscure messages. This interior has a narrative quality, like the inside of a pulpit. We have to settle ourselves into a text; nothing is written, everything re-written. We are retrospective. Even the walls are soaked with earlier tales, aborted histories.

Russian stout and blackthorn cider are secured. The rotten vegetable matter scraped from our boots. Sanctuary from the fury of event; discourse spills, like an emptied skull.

But our barman has us in his modest eye, a dangerous fever, recognised, that must be given no opportunity to break out. He swallows the rim of his lips; smooth man, alarmingly smooth, pale glow on him of moths and aspirins, weak coffee; a cupboard golem. His crisp sleeves are pinched up in garter rings; contained smile, like a thirties sex criminal. Face filled with candle-white flesh, a brandy glass of respectable mania. Obsessional cuff twitch. There is no escape from it. He has heard us, he was waiting, we have qualified. Where two men are gathered, a third is always present. Without us he would not be here: without him we could not have come.

I turned my back on the bar and hunched up; he spoke over me, to Joblard, who did not lift his eyes from the table.

'You mentioned Keats, gentlemen, what do you think of Chatterton?'

Joblard stood in front of him, in silence, hand stretched out for another pair of bottles.

'Keats wasn't frightened to borrow from Chatterton, not a bit. It's not theft, you understand, an act of generosity; you lay yourself open to a form of occult possession. You complete the other man's work, like one of those figurines the Egyptian priests used to leave in their tombs. The job doesn't end with death. And neither does it belong to any individual.'

Joblard's hand, opening for a stout, receives a postcard.

'You know the Wallis painting, of course. In the Tate, I believe. Never seen it myself; don't choose to get my feet wet crossing the river. Would only spoil the illusion. I prefer the card. It stands in the same relation to the painting as the painting stands to Chatterton.

You see, it's not Chatterton at all – it's George Meredith. Isn't that a hoot? Posing in purple breeches, shirt open to the waist, on a bed in Gray's Inn. The silly tart.

That's why the view from the window is completely wrong, St Paul's? From Brook Street, Holborn? Alignment's completely cocked up.

But what does it matter? This version is far more fun than the so-called truth. Why watch the wretched creature strain to perform when you can take home a pin-up?'

Joblard emitted a sound, between a groan and a curse, unable to wait any longer, trying to uncap the bottle with his teeth.

'I suppose you'd like the vomit and the venereal sores; he'd caught a bad dose. I'd always go for suggestion. The window behind him open just a crack. Nothing blatant.

Wallis went off with Meredith's wife. Stupid cow. He soon got shot of her. It was Chatterton he was after. He should have bought her a red wig.

Once Chatterton got to Spitalfields he should never have left. Better not to have gone at all, I agree. Should have stayed home with mother. He had the perfect set-up: plagiarising the unwritten. If it worked he could take the credit and if it failed, well, it wasn't his anyway. We've all got to find ways to distance ourselves from our own inventions.

That was the purpose of the poison. To split himself from his work, so that he could outlive it. He became a presence, manifesting himself in other men's plays and novels; spooking Francis Thompson. Dangerous ground in which to get lost.

When I first moved down here a friend of mine used to buy all his vegetables from the oldest and most decrepit men in the market. When I asked him why he said that it gave him a strange feeling to think that one of them might have known Oscar Wilde.

Load of bollocks, if you ask me.'

I am out of the door. The terror. Now they are all writers;

all rewriting the past, all being rewritten by selves as yet unborn.

I can hear the barman's voice, calling after me, 'What's your hurry? Do you want to put me in a book?'

We have to escape, swept along, no conscious decision taken; Joblard, for a man of his weight and substance, in pinstripe Bunter trousers, celluloid collar, black coat, sets out at an inhuman pace; down Tooley Street, vintners, signs, the rim of St John, Horselydown, supporting a bureaucratic glaze, over Tower Bridge, The Minories; it is not planned, we are there again.

'Come up and be dead!'

Matfellon, Hanbury, Durward. Winding it in. The heart's stomach. There is no breaking away from it. It describes us. Leaning into the magnetism, back into the belly of the secret. But we are within our limits, we are still bound by the circumference of reason; our energies, inflamed, fall back into themselves.

8

IN SPITE OF his best efforts Dryfeld was an interesting man, a man of interests: but there were dozens of other men who would have liked nothing better than to cleave that interest, to slash into it, like a blade through a melon. He was also a man possessed, a materialist. He was never there in front of you; he was always driving, forcing, rigid brow, battling on.

If you could trap him for a few hours – let us say in a car, going towards a goal he approved, the rumour of a virgin bookshop – his deeper concerns or interests would surface in a world-view that seemed, at worst, his own and, at the shallowest level, alive, vivid, cast in sharply practical language, hot, the syntax spat like rivets.

If you wanted to talk about prisons, asylums, containments – he could give you facts, anecdotes. If you wanted to split envy from jealousy, he was your man. If you wanted to talk the culture, he had seen it, swallowed it. His greed for all this was the greed of a man who has, at some point, been denied access, wholly, to these things. Who has decided to invent himself, but is not committed to the result of this brutal caesarian section.

Prognathous, he set himself to provoke the tremulous and corrupt, but essentially trivial, sub-continent of bookselling. He made it a life. Other parts of him paid for it, were subdued. He was not without his supporters, and the nature of his charm, invisible to the untutored eye, was not lost on a succession of otherwise dementedly respectable ladies. Married women were a particular target: a form of emotional prophylactic.

He was able to recognise unique qualities in the most unlikely members of the trade, but unable to give a true value to Nicholas Lane who was his Contrary, more liquid, borderless, but rigorously exact in his attention to detail. Nicholas Lane was un-inventing himself, removing himself, he was there less and less. He was generously shifting out of the human into a force of nature. Lichen under the fingernail. Coming through mere addiction until he *was* addiction. The ache without the head. The line without the shadow. Absolute damage, the critical state. A need without a source: disembodied, and of great delicacy.

Though they appeared to have so much that was common, taking the same world metaphor, the buying and selling of books, feeding the same denials, refusing meat, cooked or raw, they were the poles between which the living current ran.

The two best scalpers of their generation: cornered, poke gone, skinned, frenzy'd out. Dead kites. Rubber cheques. Sweat telephone withdrawal. Unhoused.

Dryfeld was ready to tear up the floorboards to get his cash: Nicholas Lane was ready to watch the evolution of dust in air, to wait for manclay to reform on the dry bone floor of lunar valleys.

One scalper propelled by what he had made himself, rushing into his own death mask and the other escaping, ducking behind what he truly was.

The space between them is infinite.

The narrator, seeking failure, and obscurity, as the only condition spiritually adequate to his self-esteem, is glass; he watches them, not watching, being. And can only live in them and feeding from them. Which is a state of being as full and as empty as they themselves are.

*

It's one of those short nights that go on for ever; slatted blinds sealing the cage, the dealers staring into their naked obsessions, the telescoped barrel of a gun. The suicide hour of cold coffee and alien voices on the radio. Waiting for apocalypse announcements with fatalistic calm. Reactions slowed: it's like having to tell some other body what to do, and without moving your lips; like lifting a dead man underwater.

We can all hear the scratching and tapping at the window and we all believe it – but so what, it couldn't matter less. We're cancelling each other out.

The window is so loose, the frame so rotten, that it cannot be locked: it is slowly being lifted, the blinds give a death-rattle, bones on string. White fingers tangle themselves in the slats, worms in a chinese lantern. A sick head appears; the chalky scalp, with its wet fleece, crowns, haloed in sodium, fuzzy, lemurian. Dirty hands grope for something solid. Howard Omega.

'Hey!'

No movement from his lips: he speaks out of his nose.

'Yeah!'

Nods, bleary. Whistles.

'Hey, ok. Ok, man? Ha!'

Without invitation Howard starts to pull books out of the bookcase, glance at the covers, without opening any of them, crams them back, fiercely, scoring the edges, the torn lips of trout.

'Shit! Got any decent stuff?'

Howard is like a horrible shrunken doppelgänger of Nicholas Lane; something culled from a mindless masturbatory emission. He wears a lapel badge that announces, unnecessarily, "BEAT DEATH". Howard shelters within that pun.

Nicholas Lane is visibly damaged by being confronted with this mannerless futurist madman. Who considers it normal behaviour to manifest himself, unannounced, in the middle of the night for an obscure shakedown.

He is gone deep into cellular time: so vividly living the present moment that he erases history, yesterday's books, parcels, deals no longer exist. He looks clean through Howard and the Howard behind Howard and the Howard behind that.

'Pulled a few decent numbers, man. Elmore Leonards. You wanna come down the shop? Work something out?'

Howard's nose is running, in anticipation. Good trade. Fix, score, shift: commodity exchange, *contra usuram*, let's keep currency out of this.

'Where he goes – I go,' Dryfeld grunts. 'Until we get this money split, I'm his shadow.'

Unholy twins. Waiting for surgery.

On the street they try to summon a cab. Would you take them? Two gaunt scarecrows with wild tails of rat hair; one of them bounding along, the other shuffling, as if his laces were tied; and the manic cropped Dryfeld, in despair, feeling *his* hair growing, actually sensing the stubble climbing out of his skull, shaking himself into a storm of bone dandruff.

The shop, in a narrow court once favoured by purveyors of *curiosa*, is, naturally, shut: no problem, Howard kicks the lock and the door breaks open. There's no light, that's been cut, but beyond the counter are two unemployable Outpatients defying their limits by the glow of a hurricane lamp.

One of them is working with sandpaper to erase the inhibiting announcement, "damaged stock", from the fore-edges of a pile of bought-in publishers' successes of last month. There's nothing "damaged" about them, except the stamp: and that is being swiftly remedied. The Outpatient's knees are white with the flakes of falling paper. He coughs.

The second Outpatient is hunched over a kettle steaming the labels out of a collection of oversized fine art library books. If there are easier ways to earn your breakfast, he is incapable of imagining them.

The shelves in the shop, as illuminated by Dryfeld's torch in a tunnel of unbelieving light, are rich with the direst dreck, condemned tea-chest gloom, most of the books covered in a layer of tea grains, brown, lumpy, inert. Strictly for the captive student market, yards of instant grant-bleeders.

The gelt is elsewhere.

Behind one of the stacks is a roped-off stairway that lets us down into the basement. And here the best of the Outpatients, a man whose abilities almost lift him to the rank of Scuffler, sits beside a candle, two handed, signing, with mantra-like automatism, a stack of newly minted first editions. Who would have thought that John Fowles needed to moonlight? Or that John Fowles and Dick Francis were one and the same: the left hand and the right hand.

The Ian Fleming presentations have already been taken away; to weather, overnight, under a desk lamp.

The Near-Scuffler, a former Newdigate Prize Winner, ignores us. He has seen worse things. And did not believe them either.

Dr Suk, mysterious man of business, lecturer, pornographer, liked to employ poets. He was a one man Arts Council. Liked the sense of having a court about him, the formerly great in straitened circumstances only increased *his* prestige: he pinched them tighter than ever, until they couldn't move at all. Hooked them to him in talons of need; bored with themselves, blank with fear. A comfortable pond filled with the lamest of ducks. A septic tank. Each inmate able to function: but only just. Excess of energy or imagination could only harm them. Gracious Suk, the Duvalier of Shit Street.

We waited, again, a slow tongue of light, pale through the overhead grille; the fat wheels of Suk's Mercedes block it out.

Suk looks about fifteen years old in sunshine, ninety by candle. His moonfaced benevolence, coupled with bun-sized spectacles, gave him his start: posing as the adopted child of an English Missionary to China. It was a good scam – for a while. And he played it beautifully, no hurry, easy pace.

'Excuse me, Sir, I see that you trade in Antiquarian Literature . . .' (*This to a gentleman guarding a table of tattered remnants, street sweepings*.) 'Might I have a word? Perhaps you have the time to take a cup of tea?'

Put it into print and the story screams stinking fish: but to hear him give it, the dull uninflected tones spike you, a narco-leptic nodding trance.

'Orphan sent to Theological College in the north of England'. . . (*just look at the long black coat, the damp mournful face*). . . 'Dear father's books in store in the East End'. . .(*where?*). . .'Mostly theology and church history'. . .(*groan, boredom,* **go away**). . . 'But he did also collect; er, I am not sure of the word; er-otica; very old, Sir, Japanese. How do you call them? Scrolls?'. . .(*the punter is drooling*). . .'You understand, I cannot myself sell such things'. . .(*oh no, of course, we'd look after that for you*). . .'A per-centage; we could share?'. . .(*of course, we could; very fair; 90 per cent for us, 10 per cent for you*) . . .

And when the hook goes in, cast according to the pretensions and potential of the punter; £30 on the street to £200 at the top . . .

'To get the books out of storage now.'

It always worked. Beautiful.

The taxi eased away with one sombre bowl-faced missionary orphan.

It took about two hours per hit. He could only work an area once. Morning, Camden Passage; afternoon, Kensington Church Street; Brighton, tomorrow.

It took months to put together a reasonable roll; so he claimed a degree in Accountancy and started lecturing at night school to overseas students, who knew less than he did, but who were desperate to pick up the certificates which would allow them, in their turn, to work the game in their native lands. Awarding himself a doctorate in survival studies was easy.

Smutty videos, car repair kits, fast food, student hostels, a bookshop: with plenty of flash remaindered stock, remain-dered, it must be said, without the publisher's knowledge; an easy move from a conglomerate warehouse in the sticks. They didn't have the remotest idea what they were holding : the computer wasn't interested in that kind of detail.

He'd peaked: the white Mercedes, designer jeans, pigskin jacket, his own coke dealer who'd take payment in books; which would be rapidly converted back into weasel-sugar.

The stuff doesn't come in neat plastic packets, like Miami Vice; it comes, in fast-food foil, out of the spine of a book by J. B. Priestley. A gross text, too dull for anyone to *ever* open. Dug out like a suppository: often it *is* a suppository.

Nicholas Lane takes a carrier bag and fills it with tradables, that would never now see daylight. Stored beneath the pavement, sold at night by telephone, joined to the rest of a major collection, boxed in a bank vault. Buying just enough time to sell the big one, *Study in Scarlet*.

But should it be local, J. Leper-Klamm, for a quick kill? Try £8,000. Or should they call in one of the Californian fat cats, and go for top dollar, £15,000? Brain candy. Holes in the shoe.

9

THE RECTOR filled his hat with stones. Not caring whether he bruised the straw, he dug the brim in among the flints, pebbles and broken bricks. William watched him: his eyes on the Rector's eyes, a hawk-like disinterest. The Rector, satisfied, held out the hat at arm's length, an offering.

'Seventy three!'

The boy had done it once more: replied before the question could be put.

Mr Harrison was not sanguine, could not stand against this certainty, the unencumbered act of will. How could he speak? The boy gave answers to questions he had not yet adequately framed; the necessity of asking anything at all faded; Mr Harrison twitched into silence, his goitre bobbing. But his rational, restless, measuring mind needed always to check: even on what no longer was; not understanding that the answer cancelled the question.

Rings smoothed the bland waters, running back into the dropped pebble. A hole, invisibly sealed.

Mr Harrison could not simply shake out the stones to count them, they would be lost among their innumerable brothers. He started to count, stuffing his jacket pockets, then his waistcoat, his trousers: he bulged, misshapen, a lumpy shining gentleman holding out an empty hat, a beggar.

The count had gone.

His collar rubbed against his neck, which seemed to have swollen, horribly, puffed with blood. His underclothes clung to him. Discomfort was the condition with which he was most comfortable. He understood the question the boy was now forcing *him* to answer: how many stones are *left* upon the small beach?

He could fetch ropes, perhaps summon the gardener's son, divide the area into squares, bring buckets, perhaps some sort of weighing machine could be rigged – but the ground was uneven, the tide would bring in more stones, children from the cottages could throw them into the water: he choked, he clutched at his throat, convulsive panic.

William rested his back on one of the stout black timbers of the quay, face to the mere, right hand upon the heart-bird, slowing it, holding back its reckless expenditure of time.

The jagged base of a porter bottle lay in the mud of the foreshore, catching the light. He would fire it by the force of his will, he would melt it. He saw a pattern of flame in the depths of the green, a fret; broke away, consciously. If it could be done then he did not need to do it.

'I have found a s-sign . . .' declaimed the Rector, his meat breath upon the boy's neck, wildly quoting, already knowing that the rest of the quotation was slipping away from him.
'A s-s-s-sign . . .'

It was his theory that a programme of education could only work if it be rooted in observation, mensuration, practical tests: and if the responses were kept alive, stimulated, by rapidly moving through all the disciplines, stitching them together, the whole man, healthy body; so that he would abruptly, violently, quote from the Bard, the Good Book, while William watched the birds turn, a great hand, out over the estuary, the unravelling of a dark hat.

William spoke to his fist. ' . . . And now I have lost it. Let us leave the boat on the bank and go.'

They went; Mr Harrison striding, stick in hand, white jacket, shoulder bag, listing everything, seeing nothing. The solid dark-jacketed youth always a few yards behind, heavy lids, snail eyes; his answers dragging out more fractured questions, until the Rector was done with, bodily exhaustion, breathless, ready only for the window seat, sherry wine.

They would walk for many hours, lapwing and swift, endlessly following the ragged disorder of the shoreline; stamp through the stiff grass, sometimes with a ditch beside them, hare and coypu, sometimes with a clear sight of water, the light-sucking mud; seeming to go back as often as forward, if there was a distinction, if there was anywhere to go forward to.

Beyond the quay at Kirby they met with a party of inbred and dwarfish sportsmen, guns at their feet, cattle-faced, drooling: powerful in shoulder and wrist. Unhurried, going nowhere, hands in pockets, looking out over the Twizzle; the far-off hammering of wings, the diving wheeling bird-cloud. The guns drawing in the prey; a clatter of iron filings from hollow chalky teeth.

And now as they approached the Wade, Harrison saw that somehow William had got ahead of him and was waiting at the crossing place.

The boy stands beside the long pole, sea-cross, that marks the track over to Horsey Island: the tide is coming in, the mud barely covered, but the walk is treacherous, the bubbling black ooze soon reaching over the boots, slowing, stopping the walker, who hesitates, both shores retreating, the tide now racing, deep pools on either side.

William breathes out from his mouth, slowly, a lance of hot breath; his hand on the wooden post. Breathes, blows. Across the rush of the tide, undisturbed. Out. Out of him. So slowly. The tongue of breath. Blows darkness into the lowest leaves of a solitary tree standing above the shoreline of Horsey. The tree fills, the breath rushing, unforced. The darkness of the space between the leaves closes, joins, seals the immaterial detail. Sustained: Gull's breath describes the face in the tree, takes darkness from it. There is a tunnel from the boy's mouth to the outer limits of the shore; everything else is gone.

A figure is standing on Horsey. There is an unshaped black figure at the side of the tree.

William Gull *sees*: he is looking from Horsey back across the tidal reach, across the water, at the effigies of Mr Harrison and the boy, William Gull, himself, his hand upon the post of the sea-cross. He rubs the flame in his hand, feeling a splinter drive under his nail, a memory of pain.

book two

MANAC ES CEM

10

123 Whitechapel High Street
October, 1838

My dear Sarah,

You chastise me for my incontinence of expression, you call
me "whirlwind", you say that I tell you all things but those
with which you most urgently charge me. You say that my
manner is, at once, vague, abstracted, preoccupied – and
"startling", that I am too sudden, too harsh in manner. My
dear Sister, I think you must choose your stick with greater
care before you beat me.

You compliment me on looking like a scarecrow, a
fairground dummy, its clothes flung upon its back. Nothing
fits, I grow in such starts. I wake and my arms are hanging
from the bed. I sit; my legs crawl out from beneath the
bench. My shoulders spread in the afternoon, my head
swells at night. How should I equip a wardrobe to suit such
a changeling?

And yet, and yet, all that you say has justice, guilty as charged;
but I am not wholly sorry for it. This is to describe a river by
the rubbish found along the foreshore, to anathematize
the moon because a few benighted souls run mad from its
tides, baying in the streets for red blood. I go too far: as
always, you reply!

What then of my duties? Yes, I have come to them at last!
I sit at the Temple gate and have the working of a fine brazen

monster that swallows up coin, devours paper, most heartlessly, returning little for much. I am, in short, a cashier!
I have a place in the world, not yet a significant one, but
I am truly resolute, urgent – where no urgency is required.
I sit at the door and the daylight runs from me.

We are a Christian oasis, half-forgotten, by the caravans of
the big bright world. Mr Dyer, woollen-draper, is a sober,
upright and respectable man of business. To say that is to
say all. He has, I swear it, no secret life, no life of the soul. His
only levity before us, his dependants, is habitual, and thus –
meaningless. As he enters the premises he looks around and
finding us all, always, in our accustomed places, and at the
appointed hour, he removes his gloves, opens a drawer and
declaims: 'Observe the dyer's hand!' A quotation, I suppose.
Of course, we are bound to observe anything and everything –
but that smooth white horror. He then steps into an inner
sanctum; we see him no more.

One day follows another, time passes but does not flow, as
we know it can; time is unconsummated. I rise at seven, and
dust till eight. Then do nothing, or anything there is to be
done in the morning, and ditto in the afternoon till nine.
I hand spirits across the counter to the best customers, or
those who *claim* to be our best customers, without parting
with a solitary ha'penny: those sharp-faced men whose only
claim on the hospitality of the establishment would seem to
be some special relation with Mr Dyer; a relation that involves
significant looks, the vigorous shaking of hands and
nodding of heads. Often we part with more strong spirits
than we do cloth. We had far better call ourselves *The
Black Eagle*, become a tap room, and give away a suit of
best Scotch Tweed, from under the counter, to such as
announce themselves, with a wink and a leer, as 'our best
customers.'

My dinner is taken at one, and my tea at five, after which
I have my supper, and then have till 10.30 to take my
exercise, read, write to you, &c., with little variation.

I have no news, except that my clothes are getting too small – I can't make up my mind to stop growing.

> Your affectionate brother,
> James

*

It was the shrieks at night, the horror. The gut of a cat stretched out and torn, horribly, horribly, stretched until it would stretch no more. Instead of divine music: shrieks in the night, cat-gut, the tails of horses set on fire. The voices of women, of children in pain. My shoes are off. I have walked barefoot in penitence around the body of the church, sweet grass in this foul warren – but the walls are not there. I can see the houses beyond the church; the stones will melt, the glass tempts fire. I have looked heavenward for a breeze to turn the dry pages of the trees. I wait for a fountain of stars. But the ground is parched, the soil is bitter, shards of coloured glass lacerate the skin of my feet. I tear my clothes in the brambles; I bruise my foot upon the stones; dust I rub into my hair. It cannot be borne.

Hell's hinges; Whitechapel's henges.

Hinton walked, a dialogue with fever; so cold, shaking, the blood in his face, the veins of his eyes, broken. His shirt was soaked; so many, so many pains to be borne. The blows, women reeling from the arms of their men; blood. The children, verminous; they cannot live. The streets are filled, a river of laughter, lamplight, varnished faces, oaths, the crowd has no thought, where are they going? It doesn't matter. Young girls sauntering on the arms of their men – who strain to catch the eyes of other girls. The doors of public houses open to the street. Song. Carriages. Even men of education, of substance, position, yes, they come here. Their wives allow it, are accomplice to these brutalities. They are serviced; it is done with. This red, this silken, rim of hell.

Hinton walks the circumference.

Shrieks in the night, he runs from them, towards them. So many windows; as if blind sea-birds had flown into the blank white walls of buildings. Birds buried in walls. He runs from them, on the leash of this circumference, within this invisible boundary, chews his heart. He is bound to a heat that he cannot classify.

A mad voice screaming: 'BURY THE BELL!'

Angel Alley; the cold brick walls rub his shoulders, forcing himself, he is borne in, borne on, beyond control, led out of himself, dragged out, naked, shivering. Two women in a dark doorway. Women or girls. Their hats. Faces gone into shadow, eaten. He is made dizzy by the scent, so foreign, sickly. He cannot draw breath. He wants.

As I came up to them they spoke, 'Which of us will you have?' One spoke, or both. And it was a test; a judgment I could make only with a sword. 'Which of us?'

He ran to the end of the alley; there was no way out, the walls of the buildings above him, blind windows, the sky so far away, a black wound.

Hinton, upon his knees, but will make no prayer. 'Christ was the Saviour of men, but I am the Saviour of women, and I don't envy him a bit.'

Dead windows, red lights, oven-glow, the melting of metals; the mixing of blood with liquid fires, lead and dung. Two women in the doorway.

'Come up and be dead!'

11

NICHOLAS LANE WAS one of those unique individuals who invent for themselves a new category. He was a great bookman: not a great bookseller, he could never be contacted, his stock was impossible to view – not, certainly, a great bookbuyer, his cheques were notoriously Amazonian. A great bookman, simply that. A legend. For want of others, in a small world, at a dead time.

If he could find a Hessel Street squat connection, who also supplied a runner called Nolan, he might be able to get the phone-number of an Indian accountant in Enfield, who sometimes drove to country auctions with an Islington dealer, who was rumoured to exchange sexual favours with a Clerkenwell silversmith, who shared a stall in Covent Garden with an Italian ex-football player, who had unsubstantiated Sicilian connections, and who sold books as furniture, leatherware by the yard, to a Corsican whose former girlfriend worked in the same tax office as J. Leper-Klamm. If.

Dryfeld detonated: had to be dropped at the bottom of Brick Lane, dal soup, fresh orange juice, 3 papadoms, onion bhaji, vegetable curry, *black* coffee – and the same again, please. Times Literary Supplement, all the locals, Croydon to Ongar, checking the jumbles, skin like a blood orange, hemp-veined: the man who asked for the radio to be dropped in a bucket of water. He continues his lifelong, and ever unsatisfied, quest for the perfect Bengali virgin, diaphanous sari riding on full hips, bare brown belly: who would oblige an itinerant bookdealing manic-depressive of no fixed abode, no family, and no stock exchange quotation. That was his obsession: if he could quench it he would have to find another. The Lane was the last place on earth to pursue it. He'd have more chance in Limerick Junction on a wet Thursday.

The chain broke on Nolan, not squatting, not scoring, not sleeping. The fox of memory: small ring curved in the soft flesh of his earlobe, making a bright nose in that tiny shrunken face, blooding the skin-tone. A brushed redness, redgold hair, cut short, washed into wire; tall grinning man in a flawless shirt, bleached jeans, some memory splinter of the retail rag trade, late 6oies, driver, coated, raw eyed, stimulated pupil, not seeing, unecstatic, broken, mild in manner. Nolan: spoken of, not recovered.

Remember. He would nod in greeting, stick out a hand to be slapped, to test for rain, always nodding, customers, employers, friends, family. Peddled books under the flyover, Berlin Wall end of Portobello, Friday mornings in early winter, sweatshirt, no jacket, clean white plimsolls, the sunlight hasn't lifted the fog blanket, he is standing there with damaged, torn, marked-up art books, much too active for anyone to touch, the cloth actually hot to handle, smell of college libraries, paint stripper, cow gum, defective literature trawled out of terminal cottages, 'got to be for you, man', David Gascoyne's *Short Survey of Surrealism* with the spine gone and the Max Ernst dust-wrapper cut-up and pasted onto the endpapers.

"Swift *is surrealist in malice* Sade *in sadism* . . . Poe *in adventure* Baudelaire *in morals* Rimbaud *is surrealist in life & elsewhere* . . . Albertus Magnus *is surrealist in the automaton* Lulle *in definition* Flamel *in the night of gold* . . . Monk Lewis *in the beauty of evil* . . ."

Nolan is a delivery man. Always on the run, between meets, cases to load, schlepping, no time, man; that crazed love of books as totems, unread, absorbed through the skin, has to have them around, cheques bounce, vehicle repossessed, divorce, rip-off, harm. Fly out, away, over the swamp lands; sell up in the New York rooms.

Miami; nightclerk in a Colombian massage parlor, it's very clean, whistling, scrubbing out the shower stall in his jockey-shorts. Heavy citizens. Silk suits. Hairy shoulders.

All front. Mindless. Mov-ing, baby. Julio. Angel. *Chris Craft* hijack, owners to the sharks. Cuban lift. Blowpipe technicians iced: too hot for the alligators. Bermuda Triangle scare-story video. Halter burns, shaved privates. Rectal meat-hook. The coke shoe. Gets out light, with the loss of one finger. One ring.

So it is that Nicholas Lane brings it to mind, driving alongside the London Hospital, rush hour, jerking forward on our nerves, the lit entrance, pillars, an opera, steps like a Hawksmoor church, diseased supplicants crawl in off the streets, remembers: that Nolan has been picked up in a raid, crashing, not his bust, too bad. Three years in Dorchester. Time to catch up on his Proust. View of the brewery, not Maiden Castle.

The ghost of the fox runs into a furnace of his own devising. Cover blown. Car shakes itself clear, a left, towards the river. The quadrivium that it cannot pass.

*

J. Leper-Klamm's days slipped away from him under a sick pulse of strip-lighting, bisto coloured walls; overheated, underfed, detached, secretive, head down, left handed, scribbled his tight birdfoot markings behind a sheltering curve of arm. A long bandage of dirty cuff, unbuttoned, flapped at his wrist, giving him a convalescent look; unravelled pharaoh.

Mr Klamm was not entrusted with interviews, inquisitions, investigations, not expected to break the nerve of cocky self-employed decorators, or see through intricate webs of deceit. He was not a sweater; he psyched nobody out. Within the great block of the Moorgate Tax Offices Mr Klamm was a negligible presence; he filed letters, they were never seen again.

He sent triplicate replies to defaulting company directors who had long since claimed their last expense account luncheon. His tongue tasted, permanently, of cheap glue. He was a redundancy waiting to be found out.

J. Leper-Klamm also had Europe's largest holding, in private hands, of editions of *A Study in Scarlet*. He collected no other title. His collection had cost him many, many thousands and was worth, even bled at auction, many, many thousands more. His work was a disguise. Or was it? It gave him a number on the computer, a place in the Reich. Without it he would have been so invisible that he could not have functioned. A ghost cannot *own* books, a ghost cannot lock them into rooms that only he will ever enter.

A schoolmaster at one of the educational establishments on the Indian sub-continent, founded after the model of our high-Victorian Public Schools, had given the schoolboy Klamm, cuffs flapping, dank haired, propped on his elbow, inattentive, waiting, a copy of the Sherlock Holmes Long Stories, four volumes in one, John Murray, reprint, 1952.

Klamm went through the first story, *A Study in Scarlet*, carefully, line by line, and saw no reason to go any further. He didn't read it again. But he wanted every copy that ever existed. His life was abdicated, his quest begun. Selfless Klamm, on the road to the Dharma.

It was known that Klamm lived, slept and ate, if he did eat, in a council flat in Lambeth. Nobody had visited him in it, but booksellers' catalogues were sent to that address. It was rumoured in the trade, in the way that rumours become facts, that Klamm was a man of property, with holdings in India, with interests in Whitechapel. It was rumoured, it was whispered by young men in pinstripe suits and splashy ties, the Salon of the Rejected, who spent their days gossiping at their desks, licking their lip gloss, part of the furniture of what pretended to be the leading establishment for the sale of Modern First Editions, meaning anything that looked good in a glass cabinet, it was whispered, it was mooted, the legend became fact, that Klamm owned a house somewhere, nowhere, Clerkenwell or Finsbury or Holborn, a house that was never opened to daylight, whose few articles of use had been left undisturbed, sheeted, whose rooms were filled with shelves, whose shelves were filled with books, each book wrapped in tissue paper, sealed, placed within a brown paper bag, sealed again: that there were rooms and rooms, shelf upon shelf, nothing but wrapped books, like looking into a burial ground, erased inscriptions, neat lines, the gravestones covered in stocking-masks.

It was to this den that Nicholas Lane and the Late Watson decided to follow J. Leper-Klamm.

They skulked, unlikely, among the fleecy secretaries, the green accountants from Trinity College, Dublin, the company men, suited and shaped, jogging towards their first coronary.

The evening was mockingly mild. Leper-Klamm emerged in a long black coat, tethered to several bulging carrier-bags. He would be making for his sanctuary.

When he bought a book he would ask, unfailingly polite, humble as battery acid, 'Could I trouble you, Sir? A brown bag? Thank you, thank you. And one more? Thank you, Sir. A carrier? Thank you.'

The fact that he was, single-handed, paying their salaries, allowing them to build quite amusing little collections of Uranian Verse, did not buy Mr Klamm any respect from the top of the market, Booksellers by Appointment to the country houses of England, the libraries of Nebraska. They bowed him in, they sniggered him out.

Along Finsbury Pavement, into the Square; its Babylonian follies, white brick Empires of Insurance, the architecture of fear. City Road, dissenting pocket: they dodge by railings and into Bunhill Fields. Leper-Klamm is bent over, hardly seems to lift his feet from the ground, propelled, by the wind, down well-oiled tracks; looks at nothing.

From behind Bunyan's memorial Nicholas Lane whispers,

'When he thinks he's been watched – he sings.' Nothing of that. The dull slab that marks the spot where the soul of William Blake is *not*: shaded path, railed-off boulders, holding down for ever the bloody minded, the hymn singers. Tanks of tap'd water from victims who never repined at their case. Klamm sings nothing. His lips move, a muttered monologue. 'Do you have an edition of a book by Sir Arthur Conan Doyle, Sir? *A Study in Scarlet*? Must be complete, Sir. Otherwise, condition unimportant. Thank you, Sir. Thank you.' It's almost a song.

Down Banner, now only a few feet behind him, Whitecross, and we are stopped by the sight of Hawksmoor's obelisk, St Luke's, white beacon, Nile finger. Leper-Klamm does not lift his head. Scrapes between cars, Helmet Row. Now he looks about him, draws out a key on a long piece of string.

We speed through the gate at the north side of the church, race round the path, diving into the shelter of a laurel bush, among its lacquered leaves and poison berries.

He's at the door, beyond *Micawber Machinery*. He's in. Shuttered tradesman's mansion. Beneath the needle of unspent energies, within the protected space of that roofless enclosure; sunlight lifting the blood at the rims of the broken church windows. The obelisk seems to make light, not reflect it.

Leper-Klamm has dived out of time, by a tunnel of his own devising.

Nicholas Lane has supplied him in the past; it is decided that he will go in alone. And make the pitch irresistible.

There is no bell; he knocks, he hammers, he shouts. Nothing. No Klamm. He is absorbed into the shelves of books in brown paper wrappings. He is beneath a dustsheet. There is no sound of breath from the darkened house. He is most there when the house is empty.

Nicholas Lane scribbles a message on a sheet torn from his notebook. "We have a variant first issue – trial? proof? – of S. in S. Are you interested? Nicholas Lane." And, finding no slit in the wood of the door, he slides his communication underneath, letting it float into Klamm's self-created fiction.

Nothing. The exhausted sun falls, bending the shadow of the obelisk away from the house, and the book pirates, as they squat, foxes, in their bush; casting them into a ditch of darkness.

'Do you have an edition, Sir, of a book by Arthur Conan Doyle? *A Study in Scarlet.*'

Leper-Klamm manifests. The door has not opened, their eyes never left it, but Klamm is at their side, hand in front of his face; cuff flapping, black tie loosed, shirt buttons open, revealing a severely-foxed undergarment.

'I think we could share the expense, Sir, on this occasion, of a taxi. Yes. Yes, Sir. Thank you.'

And immediately, as Leper-Klamm raised an arm, a cab, bowling down the bus line to carve up a cyclist before she hit the Old Street roundabout, slapped its brakes and squealed obsequiously to a halt.

We headed east, womb comforts, Nicholas Lane giving himself a well-deserved nose jolt. The narrator closed his eyes, to shut out the plague of street names, the undiminishing stream of high buildings. cornice, frieze, architrave, gaunt facade. He could swallow no more detail.

J. Leper-Klamm, very softly, began to sing.

12

To: Sarah Hinton   Bartholomew Close, London
                                              May, 1850

My dear Sarah,

Once again I take up my pen to defend my actions: to you who understand them best. I confess, with feelings of the deepest mortification, that I hold myself to be a fool, blinder than any 3 beetles. I am ready now to throw down my pen in sheer disgust at my incapacity. It takes me weeks and months to find out the plainest, simplest things. It is only in the last two days that I have opened my eyes to the most obvious deduction – namely, that we have a power of controlling our thoughts; if the brain thinks, it must be something else that controls this action. There is something in us, or connected with us, that makes use of our brain: something *thinks* us, that's evident. Something dictates my dictation. My brain, I am now certain, is a part, and only a part, of some greater intelligence – and my only purpose must be to let that intelligence, that mind, use me. I must serve my own will; for my will is more than my own.

I am a fool, as I said before. I have been diving into the abstrusest of physiology, and mounting into the higher abstractions of morals, to find evidence of this fact; shutting my eyes to it all the while. I deserve a good whipping for my stupidity. I could wish there was someone here to give me one now.

It is clear that if the brain is the organ that thinks, there certainly exists something that makes use of it for thinking.

The brain is the organ of the spirit, the instrument by which the spirit carries out its purposes, whether of thinking or acting. The brain is perfectly passive, just as passive as a piano. I hurl down the false dogma – viz., that living matter can act of itself. That is a grand error. Living matter, like dead, can only act as it is acted upon.

It is Physiology that must clear up these metaphysical disputes; in fact, metaphysics must be merged in physiology, as astrology in astronomy.

Don't you remember that Coleridge terms the understanding "a sensuous faculty" and exclaims, "If there be a spiritual in man, the will is that spiritual"?

It wasn't reason that led Coleridge to say that. It was inspiration. It was one of those bursts of intuition by which great poets in all ages have anticipated the discoveries of science.

I come, in the end, to this – the spirit is will and the will is holy; I must not inhibit, or stand against, its promptings. The will is law: the law is, have no law. Hold to nothing, be ready for anything. Love is the law: love and do what you will: what wills you is love.

This is a horrid letter; you mustn't puzzle your brain about it. I have sent the letter to you only because I could not send it to Margaret. The endeavour to understand oneself should bring us into closer intimacy with our Maker. I cannot strive to penetrate the depths of my being, without feeling, afresh and more deeply, the intimate relation in which I stand to God and His care for me, His love of me, the happiness it must be to do His Will.

It is agony for me to dwell upon the idea that I have gained Margaret's love only to make it a source of misery to her. I cannot vindicate myself. I wish that I had some punishment to bear that might relieve me from that thought. I have told Margaret that perhaps it is my first and chief duty at present to seek for truth; and that nothing can so well supply the kind of knowledge most useful, most requisite for me, as the seeing of mankind under all their various phases, the watching of human nature and human passions as developed under various circumstances.

I should be afraid to have any woman for my wife who would deliberately sacrifice what she considered her duty to God for love to me.

I must go to bed; but I want you to have this letter in the morning,

your brother,
James

*

Hinton, the surgeon, sat at his kitchen table, dissecting a mutton chop and carving a human ear. He ran his blade along the spine of the helix, peeling back tissue. He looked at the surface of the cartilage and saw the face of a man, in profile, something old but unborn. The secret listener to all our sorrows. A copy of Coleridge's essays on *The Principles of Method* was propped open before him. He forked up a sliver of cold meat, composing a letter to Caroline Haddon, his intended sister-in-law. For ten years his understanding with her sister, Margaret, had simmered, steamed, faltered, prosed, analysed itself; but now that he had an income, patients, a house of his own, the marriage could be postponed no longer.

The saviour of women. Whenever he thought of Margaret he wrote to Caroline. Margaret was to be his partner, the mother of his children, but Caroline would remain something more, the woman who listened to him, who had time, unattached, to follow him in his speculations.

He wanted Caroline for a sister much more than he wanted Margaret for a wife. A wife would be a part of himself, would qualify his idea of himself, but a younger sister – that was a darker mystery.

The dissection of the chop was complete, Hinton cleaned his

fingers in his beard, cleaned the beard on the lapel of his jacket; bare-necked, long nosed. The wild undisciplined eyes turning inwards, forcing the world beyond his reach into focus. No time to take up his pen; Hinton dictates to the white cell of his kitchen. To the window, the narrow close, the tree-shaded graveyard of St Bartholomew the Great, the courts of the Hospital, now swollen far beyond the priory church that gave it sponsorship; Rahere's malarial vision, the great black eagle taking him to the lip of the bottomless pit.

Flayed saint, Hinton would inscribe his testament upon the skin of your back: nail it to the door. Alleyways of false windows, painted watchers. Hinton, his mouth a spider, dictates a web of beard.

Caroline. I am justified. I am without envy, the Saviour of Women. Love is the law: do what you will. I never yet laid my hand upon any portion of God's universe that did not turn to gold beneath my grasp. Caroline. Open the shrine, that I may see my saint.

Dr Gull told me that many years ago he was walking through a field of peas. He took a few in his hand, and as he meditated he rolled them between his fingers. While thus engaged he passed by a house where lived a woman deranged in her mind. She asked him to give her what he had in his hand. He gave her two peas; she took them. The next day he called and found that they had cured her.

And what did he do then? He laughed. He might have saved from pollution the paper on which have been printed cruel books. He did not do it; but be his faults forgiven him – we have all sinned.

Caroline, forgive me. I must be scourged, my faults must be beaten from me. I will be whipped into the light of truth.

He laid his face upon the table; blood, meat, squashed to his chest, bare backed; the bulky trousers tied with a cord; over the table, forced forward, up on the toes of his boots. Beard to the cold wood; Caroline.

The knotted scourge cut into him. I will take upon me the sins of men, that women might be set free from their chains. Do what you will. Gather up the force that is in evil things, and put it to use. The sharpness of the pain-flower spreads, salt sweat running into his eyes, tears. The sweet mystery of pain.

Flesh will rise to be the spirit's minister. Praised be pain and praised be joy! Both are holy. You martyrs of Charterhouse. You blessed fathers going cheerfully to your deaths like bridegrooms to their marriage. O cut and split, this shell of skin! False restraint, self-virtue, keeping the truth away. Let bleed!

Joy is more bitter than pain and pain dearer than delight. The woman who says that sensuous delight needs some restraint is so muddled and bewildered by false ideas and false feelings that her instincts are utterly perverted and she does not know what she says. Have we not treated pleasure as a sort of harlot? See what she has become!

Only strength of passion can bring it to purity. Prostitutes have an objection to show their bodies; many will not do it for any sum. They have made a pure thing impure. I loathe their restraints. What I require, I require at your hand. Do it with thy might. Do it.

It is Caroline who unbuttons herself, long skirts falling to the floor, shift, who is naked, bright, who stands behind him, her sweet breath on his neck. The scourge of pleasure is in her hand. It is Caroline who releases the rope at his waist, whose small hand runs over him.

If all pain were seen in the light of martyrdom were not the work done? It is done, the light, the word spoken.

Her wet mouth, fevered with his prophetic heat, gobbles at him, swallows the incontinent spasms, the words falling into gasps, the barking howl of joy.

13

PAID OFF at the yard gates: Joblard is underground, at Tarxien, investigating the apsidal temples of Malta, the Hypogeum at Hal Saflieni, red ochre oracle, hive of voices around woman clay, the bell-shaped skirts; he is tapped into cool stone, the voices rush at him, reverberating certainties, he has not the speed to form the questions, split tongue; my sister-in-law, red hair, is sitting, cross-legged, with the television set, waiting. We are going to eat at the Huntsman.

A photograph of Hymie Beaker, of Buxton Street, savagely attacked, beaten. At his corner, edging towards Vallance Road. No discovered motive. Thin bones snapped, the paper of his face slashed and torn, handfuls of hair. In the London Hospital; between death and the road.

An identikit portrait of a man seen lurking, talking: horror hybrid, the features of myself and Joblard, blended. Cut and put together. Gone out of the human range.

Where two men are.

We had walked so often, after the initial incident, beyond the lorry loads of dwarf chickens awaiting ritual slaughter, the dribbling stench of fear; passing the house, trying to repair the psychic wound. But had never again seen Hymie Beaker, the tailor. Nor the red haired woman. The doors and windows bolted.

The third man had escaped.

14

IT WAS CLOSING IN on Nicholas Lane's flat; it was all collapsing. Young Kernan Quinn had been careless, he had never been anything else, but it hadn't mattered up to now. Nicholas Lane had been away so much, running about town, in such frenzy; the telephone, never stopping. Freaked: Kernan went out, took himself to the pub. He didn't drink but he had to get away from this oppressive sense of catastrophe; not knowing that he carried it with him, a shirt. It was all closing in, breathless, the dim weight of the town folding him in on himself.

All kinds of weird stuff going down, whisperings in corners, significant matches struck and blown out. The whores, unoccupied, were drinking heavily. The police, occupied, were drinking even more heavily. The grass in the corner wanted to drink most heavily, but lacked the poke.

'Can I take a look at that, son?'

Kernan ignored the Scotchman, name unknown, motives questionable. A presence, clammy in undershirt and golfing jacket. 'I think I read that one. It's a good one, that is.'

Kernan lifted the book and held it in front of his face; he hadn't turned a page since he'd sat down, the book wasn't his, he'd picked it at random, a light one, easy to carry.

'Thought it might have been something else. Not what I thought. That's the wrong book, son. You've got the wrong book there.'

'Fuck off.' Kernan spoke, provoked. Not to the Scotchman: to the world at large. 'Sod off.'

He'd heard Nicholas Lane putting the Scotchman down when he tried to run him books lifted from the Seaman's Library. He'd been on the dry and getting to be bad news all over; they'd had a whip-round to buy him a bottle of Bells and put him back on the brazier. Bury the bugger.

'Listen, son, listen to me. I think I've got something for your gaffer. Know where he is?'

Nothing. Kernan squeezed out a pimple at the edge of his nose, speculatively licking his finger. Saw from the window the taxi pull up across the road.

'Listen to me, son. Tell your gaffer to come round, tell him. Got something that's for him. His kind of stuff. God, it's strange! Fucking *weird* stuff, you tell him. Great covers on 'em. Sick! Want him to have first crack. You fucking tell him, son.'

Secretly, the Scotchman hated bookdealers, and as he sold to them, he exacted a terrible revenge. He razored out, with unusual care, one page from the middle of the text, so delicately, it was never noticed. The books were passed on, shelved, never read. In many of the great collections were books that had been emasculated and were valueless. The Scotchman liked that. It made him feel good. It never came back on him. Thinking about it, he smiled; terrifying Kernan, who was already on his feet and backing towards the door.

*

Shaving a block and rolling up, long white scrivener's fingers, the uninhibited exercise of skill; Nicholas Lane at home. The slats were down. Kernan in, hand out to grab the toke. The world at his elbow, heavy street door wide to the night, chains dangling impotent.

'I'd like to examine that Arthur Conan Doyle, Sir. *A Study in Scarlet*. If you have it, Sir. If you can put your hand on it.'

Nicholas Lane is putting his hand on J. B. Priestley, his veterinarian finger wriggling into its rectum, sure that there is just one more scrape left.

Quinn hovered, twitched, a shadow, skin tight, eyes swollen from the operation. Mind flicking on/off; the blackouts better than the rest. Nothing, man? It's great! Pains of light. Hitching up his trousers, he's so much thinner, are these *his* trousers anyway?

The phone drills in on them. Sort it out. Howard Omega. All the good books hidden in the bed, family decamped, the Scotchman might have been casing the place. 'Nice mirror you've got there, son, worth much is it? Get a few quid down the Lane for those dolls.' Pointing to the blackened fetish objects. Who point back at him, phallic blasphemy, point him out.

Nicholas Lane takes Mr Klamm into the back room, a trail, beneath lethal towers of books, slippery canyons, lightless, towards the bed, peels back the sheets. Klamm does not blanch, sniffing his goal. Lane rummages, looking for the flimsy text among scattered 3-deckers, limited editions, movables.

Phone drills again, a delivery. Can Lane hold? Omega. On Suk's behalf. Just for a couple of hours. Few mates will come round and collect. Worth an ounce or two.

As Omega walks towards the street-door, gets his foot on the step, the unmarked, but highly visible, squadcar, jerks away. It could have been post-coital anguish, the seams of Policewoman Dudley's sheer black stockings raked in a savage zigzag, takeaway chinese, hand job – or it might have been a remark. A misplaced compliment. Flushed tyres.

Omega, in his skull cage, saw nothing.

At last J. Leper-Klamm has the grail in his hands, it answers him, his life spills, everything connects. He transubstantiates; he is translated. The pages bleach to glass. The words float in sheets of crystal air. Released. Forming and reforming. "Deep in the enemy's country . . . Nothing but misfortune and disaster . . . I was struck . . . shattered the bone . . . I should have fallen . . . worn with pain . . ." Icy intimations freeze Klamm's shirt to his back.

'Have you settled a price, Sir, for this item? That might be agreeable, Sir, to all parties concerned.'

'Eight thousand, five hundred,' Lane added a quick five hundred, seeing Omega divide up the ounces on the threadbare turkey carpet.

'Would a cheque be satisfactory, Sir?' said Klamm, patting his pockets, not quite sure if the sum mentioned might not be lurking there, from his last trip to the off-licence.

Lane put a pen in his hand and for the first time in recorded history lifted his beret to mop his scalp.

The door to the room floated inwards like a vertical raft. Something was wrong; it was like looking up at a raft from under the water, some kind of distortion. It returned to the horizontal plane, crushing Omega's uplifted arm. Quinn was swearing when an axe-handle caught him in the mouth, taking out three of his upper teeth, cleanly, painlessly, with some bits of a few more. He spat blood. Stared at it, hanging from his hand.

'Get your faces into the floor. Bastards. I want all the stuff you've got. *All* of it.'

There were three of them, black stocking masks, rhino faced: two with axe-handles, the third had an axe-handle with axe attached.

They kicked over the straw laundry basket and pulled the heads off the children's toys. They smashed up the glass-fronted cabinet. They took all the packets, powders, resins, cash. They destroyed sensationalist, surrealist, gothic, hermetic, lyric and domestic literature, with a fine lack of distinction. They also gave Nicholas Lane a bit of a kicking, staving in a couple of ribs and detaching a kidney. He'd been too busy to vomit for the last week: there was plenty to untank now. Brown and sour and smelling of death.

They took the pamphlet out of Leper-Klamm's hands and tore it to shreds. If any other collector had been holding a copy it would, at that instant, have doubled in value. Nobody else was. That tunnel into time was sealed.

Perversely, at that precise moment, it flashed into the narrator's mind that the name of the man who introduced Watson to Holmes was Stamford. So close to the name of the town where their book had been found.

The heavies settled themselves, took a blow, with a vodka bottle, and waited for the yelp of the hungry phone. They knew the whole operation. Omega is made to answer every call. Every mark is told to come on round and to bring the bread.

They arrive, get their heads banged, pockets cut, skewered face down to the floorboards. After a couple of hours the chaps are holding in excess of four thousand pounds. And all the stuff. A human carpet of fowl pluckings.

The phone insisted one last time; a punter looking for anything by Fredric Brown. The man with the axe took the instrument from the wall and wrapped it around Omega's neck. 'I think it's for you, John.' Was his parting quip. They were gone.

It could have been a mob from the Brewery, sharp-end boys, down on hippie trash, could have been connections of the Scotchman, could have been a double-cross by Suk, dumping some dud stuff, could have been furies from the ether, constructed out of their own paranoia, but whoever it was they wore well-polished black boots, with thick rubber soles, and blue shirts with size 17 collars.

When the worst has happened, and all your fears are confirmed, there is a momentary sense of great calm and well-being. Sometimes.

15

BREAK THE SKIN, Quality Chop House, 94 Farringdon Road, *Progressive Working Class Caterer*; break the skin down the length of the sausage, split the pink sizzling meat, gristle and fear. Gathering the strength for an assault on the book stalls. Comfortable within this old wood booth, hands around a mug of tea; mindless detachment. Gone back.

From the street there is nothing to be seen. No other use of this time.

Inside the booth, showing solidarity with the workers by eating their sausage sandwiches, you commissars of Stoke Newington, dipping the damp white bread in a gush of crimson vinegar. Squatting on a line of power, aligned, for once, with the drift of the city. Down with the water, from the ponds, the caves of Pentonville, rush with the Fleet, beside its ditch, swept with the dead dogs towards Thames. The domes of Old Bailey and St Paul's, the hulls of tenements, the office hulks. Everything in the end floats to Farringdon Road, deaths and libraries, sacks and tea-chests, confessions, testaments. The mysteries are shredded and priced. They are offered to the guided hand.

Fed, he plunges. In on a curve, the wall pulls, a knobbled blanket, galloping wave-pattern of the eye, buildings broken up, wide-horizon seizure, sweeping from Saffron Hill to Smithfield and St Bartholomew's Hospital, rail track gleams below, a dead ladder. Now there *are* eyes in the back of the head, in the neck, the skin is clairvoyant, hysterical sharpness of nerve: touch is sight. The rippling wall threatens the eye. Eye bleeds into holistic awareness. All of the previous is there with him, he approaches himself, overtaking, rushing in, pain memories. The stalls are sheeted, roped. A lumpy bonehouse.

The MORNING STAR faces east: dim building titled to power. Red lettering, under the float of dust, making a sign but not a word. Low pulse red, receding. Where have you gone, Bill Sherman? Razor'd strips of cloud float in glass: postmortem windows.

The dealers huddle, converse in whispers. Slide a hand along the wall and penetrate the dome of Wren's machine, whale-melon vibrating in thought-star with other leviathans of the city, to swim back up Thames, the great churches, in a moment of Apocalypse, drowning human frenzy.

The rag-bundle punters connect themselves to the roped ta-bles, secret gasses, pulped trees, socks, bones, melted pine veins; vortices of hope ignite. A Siberian railway platform. Clatter of wooden voices.

As he moves, move easy, a pillar of raised dust settles into his heated absence, shadow pools soak his blistered feet. To make this wide sky London workable and safe. To take it on and make it interior. Set it in rain jungle, swallow it in vegetation, break the stones that they emerge again as calcium in the teeth of carnivorous animals. To take the buildings into the blood: as salt. This is his vision. The man becomes the building, the building floats free, shattering into other older structures, into fields of uninterrupted water.

The old men zone in on the tables. They are fierce and muted. They are driven back, abused, by the stallholder in his barber's jacket, benevolent, tufty headed; as if with pockets of condoms to distribute, with ultimate pornographic secrets. The suppli-cants are forced against the wall, rubbing their coats on the brickwork, so that when the signal is given they will be pro-pelled with greater velocity towards the naked rubble of books, their dole of half-calf. The skins of odd volumes itching to be consumed again in the cattlepens of Smithfield.

Without preamble I am seized by one of the old ones, not looking into my face, beside me, the tale that must be told, no rest from it. A trembling compulsion; not exorcism, mantraic keen-song. Over and over and over again, the argument of words: soothed, neutralised. I am witness, eyes set on the heap of books, leashed in, waiting. The story poured over me, bones in mud.

His uncle, yes, locked away now, many years, safe, a madhouse in the Surrey hills. Gestures, vaguely, with arm of raincoat lifted above the city, something blue and beyond. The uncle is freed for this time; while he is spoken of, he is with us. He hangs from the old man's mouth in white beads of spittle.

The uncle in uniform had been one of the first into Belsen. Not believing: it changed everything. The smell, hanging for miles, of death. Solicitor; new pips, cap badge, pipe, polished spectacles. Whether he became something new, or whether that experience simply cut out some spectre that was always within him, is unknown.

The full stomached officer is suddenly confronted with a vision of hell. The stench. The ground that had been blasted for ever by a mad vision, the essence of a whole people potentised, ashes cast on the wind, cursing the earth, seeding it with bone and desolate fear, taking it from use; divorced, alienated, made terrible.

He split his life. Brittle, but still functioning, he appeared on Saturdays at Farringdon Road, shabby, a fouled raincoat. Books were his world. He combed the stalls, looking for guidance, diving at Hegel, Schopenhauer, Nietzsche, Stein's *World History in the Light of the Holy Grail*, *Faust*, *The Rig-Veda*, *The Egyptian Book of the Dead*, Wolfram von Eschenbach's *Parsival*. He hoarded, annotated, quested. Snatched at discarded pamphlets, crawled under the wheels to scrape the dirt from loose signatures of *The Psychic Review*.

His obsession could no longer be fed in a single day. He disappeared, went under. Now he stood in rags, coat tied with string; now came the dreams of the lance and the cup. Wet hair hung over his face. He haunted the backrooms of theological book-suppliers with doubtful political allegiances.

And then it was done. He was gone. Back to the grove of cherry blossom: a fully-convinced Nazi. The Reich of the Final Days. He went right over. But it was secret. At first there was almost nothing to see. The theatre was gradual: black Mercedes, leather gloves, wire spectacles. Violent gestures offered to wife and family. Perversions of the cupboard. The chemical form was morphine addiction. Let it soak into what he had become, tinting his memory. He preserved and sharpened his surface routine. Until the panic spider broke through and the scream became hot metal in his throat, guttural commands stuttered in his mouth; he howled bunkers, ash, suit soaked with urine. A fist-sized microphone pressed under his chin. At the mercy of his voices. An unborn head forcing his teeth apart. Heavy velour curtains drape it, shut out the quiet suburban street.

The stallholder nods, the word is given, we tumble forward. The punters shovel up all the books their arms can hold, stacking them against the wall. Ransack the shreds of dead lives. Golden Dawn texts were found here. The Magical Revival began with planted documents. There are bricks of gold to be found beneath the tattered dross. They dig with nail and elbow. If you pause, you are lost. See yourself and it is gone forever. Too late. The hunger is dead with me.

I pick up a worn booklet in buff wrappers, from the pavement, lettered in red and blue, Longmans, 1886, Fifth Edition, *Strange Case of Dr Jekyll and Mr Hyde*. I walk away.

*

Dr Loew drove a Buick and had twin sons. It was a matter of routine for all of them on Saturday mornings to visit the Farringdon Road stalls. Like many medical men he bought books, he collected them, shelved them and one day issued a catalogue and found himself a book-dealer.

Eye-specialists favoured the stalls, gut men preferred the monthly fairs at the Russell Hotel, soothed by a sense of regularity, psychiatrists stuck with jumble sales: one wretched GP, exiled in Brondesbury Park, hoarded nothing but publishers' advance proof copies, shelf upon shelf of pink and pale blue unlettered spines, ghosts that would never become books.

Dr Loew's boys pelted each other with loose bricks from the wall, while the doctor, distracted, paced the line, examining the inert volumes, and waiting for his receptionist to announce them.

A deal was struck: in return for nothing very much the doctor agreed to conduct me into the London Hospital Medical College Museum to view the skeleton and cast of Joseph Merrick, the Elephant Man. Joblard would accompany us, with his leather bag and his sketch book.

Altruism today is beardless: above the turn of the stairs, the portrait of Sir Frederick Treves. Above a successful moustache, he hangs in oil. Fist on hip, a table of subservient bone fragments, paper in his hand, watchchain like an anchor. He stares us out.

Treves' simple act of charity had to be explained. Fiction was its truth. There were errors in the account he gave: the names of streets faltered, time flowing always in the direction of decay, improving upon a clumsy excess of detail. The truth can only be remade out of lies. What horror! A life struck out of pure invention.

His monster was found, crouching, heated by a single warmed brick. Was taken in. Other freaks were also received: you will not read their stories. They are still there. Bottles in the pathology lab, abortions floating in sympathetic oils. Their life: a circle of blinded eyes.

The story of the Elephant Man rushes at you. You cannot avoid it. Ganesa of the Last Days, Elephant Head. The place was prepared.

The chamber was ready. The unfulfilled man stalked the streets. He did not ride, contained in his hansom, like that eminence, Gull, static, stone presence, lifted above the road, seated, hands among grapes, prayer wheels spinning, repeating, infecting and sealing the padded leather space. He did not hack through victimology to the oracle. But he was after the same cup. The doctors were all tuned to the millennial flare, the century dying, the erosion of imperial certainties.

He went into the streets, into the warrens, rat holes, spikes, spielers, caves: strolling with horror.

By the collaboration of the four, Aysch, Mayim, Ruach, Aphar, was made the Golem of the fourth element. Red clay of the brickfields, complete in all his members, laid out in the field of Matfellon, in that absence, where a church had been.

Treves walking seven times through the labyrinth, from right to left, so the body grew dark, red like fire. Treves again, returning into the spiral, from left to right, seven times, around the body, through Lion Yard, Old Montague, Bakers, Buxton, Spicers, Brick, Hanbury, Great Garden, so that the redness was extinguished, and water flowed through the clay, hair sprouted, nails grew. Then Treves placed in its mouth a piece of parchment, with the secret name; he bowed to the East and the West, the South and the North, reciting the words of the ritual. He blew breath into its nostrils and the Golem opened his eyes.

At daybreak Treves addressed his creature: 'Know that we have formed thee from a clod of earth. Thou shalt be called Joseph and thou shalt lodge within my house.

Thou, Joseph, must obey my commands, when and whither I may send thee – in fire or water; or if I command you to jump from the housetop, or if I send thee to the bed of the sea!'

The chamber was prepared and the creature secured. And then it began. You can call it benevolence. You can call it good will. But that is to curse it and make it nothing.

Treves wanted a reverse alchemy. He wanted to take gold and turn it to dross. He found a being composed of radical waters, a liquid thing swimming in its own inks, lost from the light. He took it up into the cape of myth. Its world was of his making. He made himself God.

But, equally, Merrick controlled him; appearing in the seductive guise of pure deformity. Making Treves vampire; returning compulsively. Visits by day and night. Arrangements.

Treves had the Elephant Man fed on powdered gold. Gold salts had proved effective in treating rheumatoid arthritis. Was there a gold toxicity? Adverse reaction? Rashes? Bone marrow depression? Homeopathy. Physiological Physic. Treating like with like. Treating light with stronger light. Treating darkness with death. Blood dyserasias. Gold stored in the tissue for prolonged periods.

Gold salts on his porridge. The pore sweats. The chamber-pot removed, the stool examined. To turn light to base matter. The flesh made word. The golden homunculus steams. The worm. But the excrement is pure. The excitement is dry. He puts powder to his nose. It is odourless. The creature himself stiffens, a volume of letters on the table, runs his fine hand against his cheek. Rooms bright with ornaments and pictures. Is become an exhibit again: a sun statue dying in autumn windows.

Merrick was destroyed by his deliverance, taken in out of his own distress and panic, rescued; he became a footnote in the myth of Treves. He was the animal part. His own energy withdrawn and stripped. He was the exhibition of Treves' sanctity, he changed his impresario from the Silver King to the Surgeon. He was secured. He came in off the road.

He willingly abandoned himself, his unborn self, to the sensationalisation of his history. The victim drew the hand of the author over the paper: his mouth spilled, he choked on darkness.

Treves worked with surgical precision; cut away all extraneous dialogue, local colour, architecture, weather. Merrick was the nerve of all this: and it was at the cost of his own existence.

He could not be forgotten. He was umbilically attached to his creator. Uninstructed, the Golem, like one mad, began running about in the Jewish quarter of the city, threatening to destroy everything.

He was the missing chapter of Edwin Drood; but Dickens shied back from a deformity that he might have shaded but could not quite turn to sentiment. There was a clairvoyance of ugliness that frightened him. The sideshow freak becomes Presence. And what had been his life was left to enter the stones, to move away among dim tree heights, to describe the rim of the missing church of Mary Matfellon. A taint in the colour of the hops.

He sat where he had sat before. And now there was no temperature; no veil over the nakedness of his face.

As we approach the glass cabinet we walk into his skeleton. The cabinet is set at an angle in the most obtuse corner. A phrase is present, not spoken by any of us, left in the room: *'inside it always smells like rotten marble.'*

Climbing towards this secret room, by steps, winding into the vermiform appendix of the caecum. Forbidden steps, at hieratic distance, enlarging our stride.

As we approach the skeleton cabinet, we approach our darker selves. Joblard's meat outline is imposed on the twisted bone armature. My face stares out from the skull cast, taking on an inherent mongolism of dim oils. A caul of opaque skin hides me from the light. The bones on Joblard's suit are aboriginal lime. The Elephant Man's peaked bee-keeping hat, his net, keep out the angry eyes. His collapse at Liverpool Street Station, steam cathedral, walkways, girders, high forests, hat torn from him, the weight of oppressive Great Eastern Masonry.

Bury the bell! Flinching. On this site: the Bedlam yelps, the cages of straw.

He is rescued. A portrait of himself. A specimen. Joseph Merrick, Pope. The church model upon his hand. Entering the tarot of blasphemy. Rioting bone coral. The hat. The church in all its detail.

The glass is a mirror.

So the circuit is completed: the eyes of the audience are brought to this place to look into themselves, to look out, from the painted shadow of what a man was, to the three dark shapes crossing the floor to join with him, in one unbroken moment.

*

Across the generous boulevard, Whitechapel Road, and into the Blind Beggar; stopped down, thirsty. We are looked over and ignored. There's a few of the chaps in from Brady Street, so the Brick Lane mob stay clear. But we are only amateurs of ullage, don't count: drink up, move on. No claim to any territory. 'Arright, John?'

The chaps are talking overtime, but make it look like a bank job. Hunched in dynamic tension, not a casual hair, water slicked. Knees that don't fit under tables. The light is stained, the street drifts back, snatches of warm breath.

'Hinton, for me, is the key figure. The whirlwind, energising principle. He puts it all up in the air. But he's crazy, he's out of himself. He erodes his boundaries; he spills. And it's up to others to interpret his work, to take it on and carry it through.'

Joblard is used to these uninvited monologues; they are fed into his well-earthed intelligence. He doesn't have to reply to them; he returns some fragments of his own, precise and accurate tales, seemingly unconnected, but burning the time until it is gone, the poison absorbed. He has the gift of turning nouns into verbs. He makes them *move*.

'Did you ever read Hinton's son, Howard? *What is the Fourth Dimension*? Published 1887, of course. It was all there, all coming to the boil. Howard was completing one aspect of his father's work.

James Hinton says, "Will my friends try after I am dead, for I cannot do it myself . . ." He says, "It was too much for my brain, but it is by the failure of some that others succeed . . ."

He says, "Either I had a second self, who transacted business in my likeness, or else my body was at times possessed by a spirit over which it had no control, and of whose actions my soul was wholly unconscious."

He left the harpoon on the table. He forced other men to take it up. It's that mad, self-heated, excitement that connects with the real but cannot translate it into action. No action would be enough. It was gone when he said it. He saw the contrary. He cancelled himself.

But Howard, the son, hooked onto just one part of Hinton's pitch, the acts of time. He described a model system of lines, nearly upright, sloping in different directions, connected to a rigid framework. He proposed that this framework be passed through a horizontal fluid plane which stretched at right angles to the direction of the motion. There would be the appearance of a multitude of moving points in the plane, equal in number to the straight lines in the system.

We have got to imagine some stupendous whole *wherein all that has ever come into being or will come co-exists*, which, passing slowly on, leaves in this flickering consciousness of ours, limited to a narrow space and a single moment, a tumultuous record of changes and vicissitudes that are but to us.

So it's all there in the breath of the stones. There *is* a geology of time! We can take the bricks into our hands: as we grasp them, we enter it. The dead moment only exists as we live it now. No shadows across the landscape of the past – we have the past, we have what is coming; we arrive at what was, and we make it now.

We give ourselves up, let go, stalk up on ourselves unawares. We walk into our own outlines; we are there before. Howard is become his own father.

He articulated his father's uncompleted argument. We service the dead. Without him a piece of the father would have disappeared for ever.

You can't get off that curve. It's like old Dick Brandon. The family eating their breakfast in a back-kitchen at Bow are already dead, the Peenemunde rocket launched from German scrublands. The patriarchs are scattered on the roof; it is with them as they go about their business, it is lead in the skirts of their coats. They might as well take a ladder, climb onto the parapet and wait for their death.

Until we can remake the past, go into it, change what is now, cut out those cancers – we are helpless. We are prisoners, giving birth to old faults, carrying our naked grandfathers in our arms.

What Hinton said, Gull did. Hinton claimed, "Prostitution is dead. I have slain it. I am the Saviour of Women." But it was Gull who took the hansom-cab as a time module: one of Howard's diagrams made actual. He floated in a solution of time, lifted above the horizontal plane, out of it, not that crudity of arriving, not anywhere; realising, embodying, all those potential moments of will.

The great synthesis travels in a sealed cab. Stars move across the pitched roof, the coracle lid: at the velocity of Gull's breath. Compressing his time. Making incisions, making sacrifice. Gull, the literalist, made act, made complete, *did*. Or Hinton would have been nothing.

Gull, the ironist, not needing to believe, oversaw the slaughter of five women. Coldly; unattached to his actions. Buried one threat. Earthed one terror. Made sacrifice that the new century could be born. He aborted his own future.

He was a victim. He could not escape the acts he had to perform. The will of the victims was as great as his own: rushing together into annihilation, each serving the other.'

Joblard now was sketching rapidly, black contours, rib and vein, the heart's heart, the labyrinth of the secret city, the temperature-graph of the dying stones: neutralizing the spread of madness.

We made our way back, Hanbury, Spital, Woodseer, to the brewery gates. A visit. It is my instinct: never go back. To return is to remake what is. But Joblard, having no past, cultivates the pieces of the immediate that can still be reached.

The gift of friendship, the knack of making demands: it is kept alive.

The ullage men are dozing behind their guts in the concessionary bar, only slightly inhibited by a made-up front-office man drinking with two plumbers and a girl they have brought back from the Seven Stars. They have connections, involvement with doubtful invoices, the juggling of delivery notices. Lightweight suits like oil slicks, cheap cigars. They punctuate their remarks with sudden touches on the woman's shoulders, leaving incipient bruises in her soft flesh. They are pouring doubles into her, promising the full tour.

'How's the old feller, then? Still around?'

'Dead. You didn't know? Six months back. Dead and buried.'

'Old Eves, he'd been working on it a long time. It's what he was waiting for.'

'Fuck Eves! He's still running around, the old wanker. He'll be dying for the next thirty years. He'll see you out, mate.'

'Who then?'

'Brandon. Cut him open, didn't they? Full, mate. Every fucking inch of him. Packed, he was. Cancer. He was drinking in this bar on the Friday – they had him six feet under in Tower Hamlets by the Tuesday. Suit him there, nobody checking up on him. He never changed, like a skeleton. No teeth. Finished up his pint, didn't he? Got another one in, didn't refuse. But he never fucking drank it.'

The chaps, the well-connected trio, take the girl out, tip-a-toe on stilt heels, laughing, over the cobbled yard of the cooperage.

'Come on, boys. We'll follow them.' Ullage boss as voyeur. 'Might get some fucking leftovers.'

Down the dray-walk, into the stables, a suggestion of rats at her ankles, the girl obligingly lifting, shaking, her tight skirt;

a run in her stocking. The exact extent of the damage to be assessed by the man from the front-office.

Then by tunnels and walkways, a route that involves many ladders. The girl follows one of the plumbers, the office man at her rear, closely guarding against any danger of her falling by resting his manicured hands on her buttocks. They pass gleaming tanks, skimming baths, hoppers; they enter the cold store, along Hanbury, chilled porter, the shunned corner, the ground where the body of Annie Chapman was discovered, turned out at Dorset Street, "the worse for liquor and potatoes." The plumbers go no further, not worth the candle; a tap and a bucket. They sit on the stone floor, passing the bucket between them, sharing a song.

The office man wraps his jacket around the girl's shoulders, an overcoat, scarlet lining; manages at the same time to disengage the straps of her dress. He warms her with a long pull at his flask.

Our quest is unfocused. We join the plumbers on the deck. Seminal promptings frozen; we float once more in the direction of decay.

'She'll bite it off!'

'To the brim, John. Fill her right up.'

The bucket carried unsteadily back; it spills, soaking the plumber's overalls.

A scream.

The plumber sits up too suddenly, gashing his head on a brass tap. Blood down his cheek. A scream that freezes us to our shadows.

We blunder. There are so many doors, ladders, steps, dead ends, blind passageways. We dip under pipes, lacking Brandon the guide, the rat among secrets. A long floor, out of the darkness, grain over boards, high arched ceiling; a pulsing of machine breath, nerve dials.

And in the powder, on the floor of this glass-wall'd chamber, a line of footprints, leading our eyes to the man, head on his knees, nursing an aluminium pipe.

The girl, now virtually naked, jacket slipping from her shoulders, hurls herself against a window; it shatters. She drags her wrist backwards and forwards across the jagged glass edge, screaming madly: bands of light from the shuttered roof stripe the nave, white dust floating in immaculate columns.

16

To: Sarah Hinton   8 Finsbury Square
                                                  July, 1861

My dear Sarah,

Where do you think I am now? I am at Dr Gull's. I have
taken up my abode here for a week or so, to do a paper with
the Doctor, the one we were talking about before.

I was so filled with my ideas, swollen and exultant, absorbed
in my schemes and projects when I saw you, that I did not
even tell you where you could find me.

I want time for the thoughts to mature, so that they may
present themselves in fit shape, and not need to be worked
up.

The Doctor listens, an owl in a green waistcoat, bottled
in his window seat, the light behind him, his feathers all
on fire. I cannot read his expression, his approbation or his
censure. I believe that he looks at my chair and sees nothing.
I am invisible – but my words go for him like hornets, and they
sting!

His right hand always resting on his abdomen, feeling every
breath as it escapes, so infernally calm, so contained, with all
the complacency of an expectant mother. Those heavy cater-
pillar eyebrows! That remote eye! He seems to have welcomed
my train of thought before I have launched it from the platform.

And now he is such a great man in the world, his wife and

family live at Brook Street – his old surgery in Finsbury he maintains as bachelor quarters, so that we can talk without disturbance; talk, talk, talk! I am sure that I weary him, but he gives no sign. Indeed it begins to come on me that I do no more than save him from the exertion of articulation, of defining, working down to what does not need to be said. The smoothed cap of hair! The high stiff collar! The very portrait of a successful physician. He has painted himself and disappeared into his own likeness.

But I owe so much more than I can tell to Dr Gull, our walks together, each morning, the divisions of the city as yet unpolluted by the traffic of mere business. And our walks at night into the dark heart, the gutters, the veins of corruption. So much of the inspiration for *The Mystery of Pain* lay not in secluded study or in quiet contact with nature, but in the back streets and slums of Whitechapel. Evil, Sarah, is a stained glass window with a glowing reality behind it; it is radiant with martyr and saint, with the divinest meaning just beyond our sight.

I thank God there is so much ugliness and evil. I clasp evil and wrongness to my heart; they are life, they are God's tenderest love. He says to me in them, 'Look, my child, and tell me what I am doing; 'tis painful to you at first, but you will love it when you see it.'

The thought of the mystery of pain is the seeing our life again as a Fluxion. The feeling of pain is an element brought into the self-form by isolation. This I have suffered, but not for my redemption. It is not until we look upon pain as a willing sacrifice that it becomes pure good. I have refined self in pain and refined pain until it is a force in my work. It was of use, no more. The highest good of everything is its making possible a better thing, a thing not possible except for it.

I was given a seed and when I loved it I was bidden to bury it in the ground, and I buried it, not knowing what I was sowing. That joy is more bitter than pain, that pain dearer than delight.

Sarah, we have gone so far together. Your offer this afternoon clears my path. Here is the work: to gather up the force which is in these evil thoughts, which now we merely feel as pain, uselessly, save as it makes a tension in our hearts that must gain its relief and expend itself in life at last: to gather up the force and put it, directly, to use.

I have seen such sights. A man may have reason to say he has found a door, and not a wall, although he can open it but a little way, and he has very scanty ideas of the space into which it leads. You will remember how utterly I must be unable to do justice to what I want to say.

But I hear the Doctor's tread, he is not asleep, though he is never, as I am, troubled; restless, turning. I do not disturb him with my work. I am quite silent, I assure you, letting slip only the occasional moan. The heat of my thoughts, the intemperance of my argument, must not be allowed to break in on his meditations, which are unseen, water running beneath water. I will restrain my hand and let my words go free, where they will, from the window and out into the ignorant and uncaring streets.

Your brother,
James

To: Caroline Haddon   8 Finsbury Square
                                              July, 1861

My dear Caroline,

I was at De Beauvoir Square this afternoon, and Sarah said to me, 'Make haste and write your book; I will pay for the printing of it.' I went to Dr Gull in the evening, and mentioned it. 'Tell your sister I will divide it with her.'

I have just put down my pen and sealed a letter to Sarah, but I cannot rest, the Doctor is occupied, and there is so much, so very much to be said; please forgive me if I say just a little of it to you. It is not enough to leave these things half-born. Nothing can be that does not act, or be except by acting.

The world is ruled by thought, but no one knows what will come of doing.

And yet from a little commonplace idea I have started on a train of thought that has almost revolutionised my "holdings" on many of the most interesting and important subjects of thought, especially to a physician. My new ideas may be true or false, or rather, in great measure, they must be false; but that is not the question. They are new and mutually dependent, and inasmuch as they have flowed from an obvious though unrecognised truth I think they may contain the elements of something valuable.

But I was going to tell you where I have finished; for I must have done now, since it is impossible to go any farther. I have at last embraced the revolutions of the planets in my investigations, and propose to wind them up with an inquiry into the centrifugal force. You will smile, but I speak in earnest. I have either lighted upon a great fact or a monstrous fancy. If it be the latter, I am content: you know my opinion as to the part which error plays in the world. I don't aspire to any higher honour than to do my work.

If my ideas be correct, and it may be partly so, I have made a step towards solving, not the essential mystery, but the "mystery" of life. I want to meet with some first-rate mathematician and astronomer just to put him a few questions as to the centrifugal force, and then I would positively abstain from further pursuit of these subjects for the present, and would patiently retrace my steps, and sit down deliberately to mature the speculations that have crowded upon me, and revise and purify what I have written, which amounts to upwards of four hundred closely written foolscap pages.

Do not suppose I set such pursuits of science in comparison with moral aims. I don't hold that man is an observing or reasoning animal, or that any amount of intellectual exertion or scientific attainment can be pleaded in excuse for the neglect of duty. The will is the man, not the intellect.

Perhaps I over-reach, attempting to circumscribe and set limits on the unknowable; "unknowable" because to know would be to go beyond self, beyond limits, dissolve boundaries, give voice to that which is forbidden, a blasphemy of the truth.

But whatever fails, unseen ends are served; better ends than those which failed.

Think what a work had to be done! The price of my vision and of the madness it brings will have to be paid. It must be. It was not possible to have the whole world turned round and be quite different, and to see the assurance of its being good and not evil any more, without being driven back on oneself, and the penalty will come, and not alone.

Others can do in cold blood what genius does in pain and crucifixion. Genius is the inability to keep out Nature; it is the woman in man. The pivot in the turning world. It must be crushed. That is part of the work, its function. Uncrushed, the work were not done.

Genius asks no questions, follows Nature blindly: to licence, or madness. Nature repudiates man's goodness in so far as he is not one with her. Too much denial, too many restraints! Nature says, 'That force you are wasting I want to use through you.'

Genius sees the invisible. Men of genius are the women of the race. Genius is the positive denial of self, as asceticism is the negative. Genius-work has in it what cannot be done by will. It is the right leaving-off, abdication of control, inhibition of reflex. That is what heaven is called, a ceasing from labour.

The act must be half unawares, on the spur, not deliberate. A new thing; no conscious repetition of a thing done before.

I will do it. And I leave my justification to you.

As always, your friend
James

*

When the light was clean they kept to the heights. Water table. Windmills. Grazing cattle. Hinton's sleep took him out of the city by routes that could never be found. Hills lifted from Islington, sudden as icebergs; meadows, streams. The cavernous streets cracked and let him into a tainted Arcadia. He walked through dockyards and wharfs that became forests; sunlight shafted the clearings with an estranged symbolism. He dipped hand in clear fountains, but he never drank from them.

Always, they returned. Their backs to the sentiment of open landscape; those fields were blank pages. They spun on their heels to face the excitement of the city's unskinned heart, its glittering towers and monuments. The moment was postponed, the pleasure sharpened. But not prolonged. They plunged once more by Percival Street, by Goswell, St John, Farringdon; the same tracks, towards the known enclosures, the sanctuaries of power. The city was a museum of itself.

Morning of blood and daffodils, a frenzy of small birds kicking the soot from an irregularly roof'd escarpment. Gull plods, calm, canonical, satisfied: a man who has made love to his wife minutes before setting out; unbathed, replete, extending his sense of well-being to the new day.

He pokes, he prods; he trifles with a heavy cane.

Hinton steams, drives like a piston, the nap of his hat brushed the wrong way, ungloved, stopping, staring wildly about, surprised, unsettled, strung up, a bundle of odd volumes under his arm. He is Holmes returned from the Falls, revenant, born again, "strange old book-collector, his sharp, wizened face," clutching *The Origins of Tree Worship*.

Fasting Hinton scorns the Quality Chop House; Gull's juices bubble with disappointment. Hinton makes prophecy from the moisture on the moon of his fingernail. Onward! Blows back the scarf of cloud. Sir William contents himself with digging a splinter of dry mustard out from his raw one-day beard. Lags, noting his companion's heel, ground down like a molar dieted on pebbles.

'You are heart-dead now,' said Gull, 'I was summoned to give a second opinion; I informed them that my opinions were of necessity final. They were, in fact, not opinions at all – but judgments, made of long experience and observation. I am the ultimate court of appeal. It will cost you one hundred and fifty guineas, my dear sir, to learn that you are already a dead man. Arrange your affairs.

The shock finished him.

The creeping acolyte, who was in attendance, hovered like a dung fly, with his "Lord Arthur requires . . . Lord Arthur demands . . ." Damp-pitted student, scarcely in control of his own bowels. Couldn't answer you the day of the week.

"I have done nothing, Sir William," he bleated.

"Well, at least, you have done that right," I told him.
Before I sent him packing.

"Do not shelter me," Lord Arthur mumbled, "I want the true state of things, Sir William."

"You are heart-dead," I replied, "the rest follows. We have done our business."

"Sir, I have burnt my boats. I listened to the councils of lesser men. They led me to hope that there might still be time. I have a wife, a young family," he whined in my face.

"Lord Arthur, your time has been long overdrawn. I came upon a phrase in an essay promoting that grievously misguided poet, Thomas Chatterton, 'You cannot burn your boats when you live inland.' Certainly it's not a trick for the living; but the coffin is the only craft that you will sail in. Good-day to you."'

The parable was spat at Hinton's neck, wasted.

They entered the old Templar enclosure by St. John's Gate; Gull, flushed and hieratic; Hinton, dragging his foot, trenching the dust.

Cattle were driven in front of them, sullen, loose bowelled, within sight of the slaughter pens. The gaudy shop-signs promised tripe, offal, meat fresh from the hoof. Grinning butchers leant upon axes. Meat dressed like confectionery. The stench of fear. Sweet stink of guttered flesh. Pelt, horn and tail bubbling in the vat.

But the high clear voices of young boys rehearse the blessings of this newly minted morning. From St Bartholomew-the-Great a wedding choir shapes its cone of glory: sea-gulls under twisted basalt columns.

'Such purity of sound!' cried Hinton, 'such glimpses of the real in the apparent. They celebrate the woman in man. It is surely the heartless and unblemished song of the *castrati*. The true affinity of sacrifice is with rapture. But what a price! Can it be worth it? Manhood plundered!'

'It can. We must eat.'

Gull took Hinton by the elbow and drove him, the shortest course, down the central aisle of the great meat cathedral of Smithfield, under the sign of Absalom & Tribe Ltd, under the hooks and lanterns, through the beach of blooded sawdust.

This night place; herds arriving, muffled in darkness, dressed for the table by morning; thick scent of fat clings to the clothes, buckets of dark ornaments, black and purple, glistening pebbles of skin. The animal inside-out. They walk into the stomach of an upended cow; they are lost in its iron ribs, milk turned by terror into acid.

Gull's fast is soon broken.

They join the bloody-coated slaughtermen in Brown's Restaurant; plain wood, long mirrors enshrining the market, forcing the doctors, the butchers, the priests into a single moulded frame; hot breath clouding the detail, a trellis of fruits and grains.

Hinton takes no more than a mug of scalding coffee, his thoughts now so completely undressed that they spill, pus from an open sore.

'I know it was those shrieks at night, like the baying of cattle, helpless, pointless, already dead, those hell shrieks, when I lived at Whitechapel, that banished the self from me. A horror came over me, which remains undiminished after all other experiences of horror: it was this above all that determined the shape of my life.

I am a Knight of the Holy Ghost: I felt it as we entered the gates of this city within a city. I am born of the water and the wind.'

'A fool,' replied Gull, lighting a cigar, black as lung blood, 'is known by the littleness of his folly. You, my friend, swollen on excess, are like a dog so maggot-filled that it seems to move of its own volition, to crawl on its belly. Every thought breeds three illegitimates, every illegitimate another nine. There will be so much of you that you will be altogether gone. You are the book, chapter and verse, of your own Apocalypse. I must forcibly restrain you – to keep you with me. I hear a voice crying, "Cover him, crush him, keep him down."'

Hinton is lost in a cope of blue smoke, beheaded, arms jerking; plaintive.

Gull drops ash onto a wafer of white butter, admonishes, 'Hurt not the oil and the wine!'

Hinton slumping onto his arm; crushed in his pulpit.

'We have come to the end. It was too much for my brain. I am so exhausted that I seem scarcely to believe in anything before me.'

He is surrounded. Gull's three-button coat curtains him, the power of lead, and behind, unseen, Gull's full face, reversed, King of Pentacles, bull-heads upon his shoulders, rising, black and ferocious, from the rim of his chair.

But still he cannot attain silence.

'I am on the side of the bad. I hate the good with their meagre sympathy and their fermented intelligence. I acknowledge the woman in man, the meaning of the prophecy, that which has been spoken: we fulfil what we discover. We reinvent what has been, so that it becomes what is.

"The woman was arrayed in purple and scarlet colour, and decked with gold and precious stones and pearls, having a golden cup in her hand full of abominations and filthiness of her fornication: and upon her forehead was a name written . . ."

'"MYSTERY, BABYLON THE GREAT, THE MOTHER OF HARLOTS"'

Gull was leaning forward, his head resting upon his fists, dull mollusc eyes, unblinking, a stone.

'Just so. Mystery, Babylon, The Mother. The shriek at night. The midnight harlot's curse . . .

And what does God accept as a sacrifice? See what He has accepted from the harlots! See the enormous power . . .

The great sacrifice must be made to cast out prostitution. The cure is in a woman-sacrifice, nothing else or less. For what is prostitution but a stupendous woman-sacrifice? Shall there be less sacrifice in the world when prostitution is no more? Not till heaven and hell change places!

Prostitution protects and maintains the prudery of respectable women. This is too high a price for virtue. Women cease to be women while they maintain prostitutes to lie with the beast in man, to milk the poison from our desperate sense of mortality. Man cries out, in fear and shame, "I must die!" He shrieks aloud even as he bucks and rears upon his harlot-lamb, dies as he spends.'

'No woman,' remarked Gull, 'is a duchess a hundred yards from a carriage.'

Hinton stared at his hands, seeing claws, knotted, sweating.

'How little comes of this rancid philosophy, from the softening influence of literature. How little is known of prostitution. We must break Satan's subtle chains – the self-life. Roll back the heaviest stone from the sepulchre. And who shall perform this? An angel clad in white with heavenly lustre on his wings.'

'*His?*' enquired Gull, 'an angel with an interest in moral philosophy, with a shovel beard, and a nose like a stallion's bulb?'

'Prostitution is dead. I have slain it. A woman has possessed the talisman. But I am the Saviour. I have found it out. It will be two hundred years before my work is understood.'

'My friend,' replied Gull, 'you are overmodest. You think of death as a purely human idea. Death is a dimension, like time. Only time can redeem it. You have circumnavigated the theory but you cannot *describe* the action. The act is to be acted. Or it is nothing.

The sacrifice will only be complete with the willing assent of the victim. *That* time is almost upon us, the time beyond words. If we mistake it – it will not return.'

He breathed: a moist cloud upon the mirror, an eye of breath that slowly contracted, revealing the face of a young woman, floating in the silver; a woman standing behind them, with no hat or bonnet. They did not turn. Red knitted cross-over around her shoulders, dark hair, very young, linsey frock, black velvet body.

A smell of violets, left too long in water.

Gull wiped the glass clean with the back of his sleeve. The ouline of his hand, framed in a shield, remaining. A trowel of earth.

'The days of the Antichrist are come. Know now that I am appointed time's abortionist.'

17

MIDSUMMER: the shortest night. The year on its side. Joblard is to marry. To make that act, that avowal: St Bartholomew-the-Great. The Chemical Wedding, *sponsus* and *sponsa*, merging in song, twisting around the columns of that stone forest; celebrated here in the blending of russian stout, *nigredo*, with dry blackthorn cider. The risks crowd us, cackle; magpies at the window.

Birds spin into hats, they disguise themselves. We suffer the resilience of the silver-workers, lion spirited, boisterous, loud upon pavements: the Hat & Feathers, corner of Goswell and Clerkenwell Roads. Broad challenging frontage, fresh paint and pillars of red Peterhead granite, gravestone.

Naturally, we do not talk of these things, the things ahead. Does the unspoken, for the first time, put a tremor in Joblard's hand? Hardly. Rolling a cigarette, damaged finger in a leather stall.

Pints first, begin slowly. Change on the table-top. Joblard running three coins between his fingers. Blackmail the ferryman. Ungrounded bribes. Don't say it! Take all the time because there is so much coming at a rush, more than the short night will hold.

Without preamble, I plunge.

'Accepting the notion of "presence" – I mean that certain fictions, chiefly Conan Doyle, Stevenson, but many others also, laid out a template that was more powerful than any local documentary account – the presences that they created, or "figures" if you prefer it, like Rabbi Loew's Golem, became too much and too fast to be contained within the conventional limits of that fiction. They got out into the stream of time, the ether; they escaped into the labyrinth. They achieved an independent existence.

The writers were mediums; they articulated, they gave a shape to some pattern of energy that was already present. They got in on the curve of time, so that by writing, by holding off the inhibiting reflex of the rational mind, they were able to propose a text that was prophetic.

Doyle encodes the coming sacrifices, Stevenson's *Jekyll & Hyde*, in that predetermined calvinist language, describes what is almost at hand – the escape of the other, the necessary annihilation of self. The Whitechapel Golem, unsouled. There were so many figures, conjured essences, loose among the traps – unfocused, undirected. I don't know whether they reported them or created them.'

I fumble for a notebook. Not sure if I've lost it. The urge towards saying; knowing that what is said is false, thickens the line of truth. The ill-shaped sentence bruises the past. I need a quote from Francis Crick.

'"*If, for long periods of time, one could prevent the two sections of the brain communicating with each other, one could perhaps convince one brain that it was in the same body as another brain – in other words, one could make two people where there was one before. An area of research that is likely to lead to interesting consequences.*"'

'Hymie Beaker,' Joblard replied, sliding across the first chaser.

'Also,' I couldn't stop now, 'on Radio 4, February 19, 1969, he predicted the creation of man/animal hybrids.'

'Too late. We've already got those,' said Joblard, as his mate Jack, hovered over us. 'The Third Man: part musician, part crocodile.'

Jack presents himself, initially, as an alien life-form. The light from the streetdoor shines through his grey raincape. Beads of sweat trickle down his scalp. His thick glasses are misted over: he is eyeless. His arms are lost within the wings of the cape.

Jack grinned at us: not extinct, obsolete.

But he was so amiable, so lacking in nervous speedy aggression of manner, that I was forced to assume a terrible stubborn fury beneath. Jack made no imposition, needed to assert nothing. More than any human I had met he obeyed Nietzsche's gnomic instruction: "become what you are."

Strong-throated, Jack cleared his glass; listened. A vital witness, neutralising the possible escape of the third side, the necessary stranger, always present when two men are talking. Jack sealed the triad. A new benevolence.

I truly believe that if we could have kept him we could have changed fate. The sacrifices would have been annulled. The shriek in the night, by this addition, earthed.

But the fret is on, it's compulsive. One of those times when it has to be said.

'Rimbaud, Verlaine. Went over the ground. Verlaine said, "*As for London, we have explored it long ago . . . Whitechapel . . . Angel, the City . . . had no mysteries for us.*" He said that the City had "*the atmosphere of a machine-shop, or the interior of a heart. All the heroes are to be found there.*"

And this is simply the truth. They are there as guides – the poets born and dying at the old gates of the City.

Chaucer, Keats; Milton, born at the sign of *The Spread Eagle*, his father had another house, *The Rose*. And they are there in the stone effigies, the Moloch facades. It's the most darkly encoded enclosure in the western world. Bad magic, preconscious voodoo.

Rimbaud and Verlaine were, at that time, the great time for them, the time of their time, into that inhuman sex heat coupling, "total derangement", that was occult in intention as well as effect; the will of Rimbaud and the compliant sacrifice of Verlaine, reversing and twisting, exchanging, *animus* and *anima*, reading each other's dreams, spine snake dramas, double-helix, pain. The black acts. Like Crowley and Victor Neuberg in their talentless variant. *"They were full of eyes within."'*

The evening was rancid now, our glasses slid in pools of sweat across the table. Our arms stuck to the chairs, which creaked as we moved; faked pornographic sighs.

'I can *feel* the fucking going on,' said Joblard, with relish. 'Does it take two to occult fuck? Or more?'

Jack groaned. I drove on, undiverted.

'Verlaine saw it, but didn't do it. He projected a *"ferocious novel, as sadistic as possible, written in a very terse style."* But couldn't carry it off; gone, swallowed, finished, back to the domestic teat, hungry ghost begging for absolution in the skirts of the church, breathing old farts.

From these acts only one man emerges. The other is eliminated, engorged. Verlaine was bloodless, sucked dry as paper. He was wholly necessary, an equal partner, but he never emerged from that room. What he had went over.

Rimbaud was reading, British Museum, diving into Poe, into magical primers. He claimed that writers are *"the mirrors of gigantic shadows which futurity casts upon the present."*

That's it exactly. *"In everything any man wrote . . . is contained . . . the allegorical idea of his own future life, as the acorn contains the oak."* Yes!

They were pulsing, they were open. They roamed, every day, out along the river, into Whitechapel, Wapping, Ratcliffe, Limehouse. Entering wilfully into that fiction.

Rimbaud's occult awareness was so intense, he was burning his own time so recklessly, all or nothing, that he described more fiercely than any other man, then or now, the elements of the Whitechapel millennial sacrifice. And by describing, *caused* them. They were said. They had to be.'

Jack cast a baleful eye on the notebook, but at that moment

he would rather drink than talk. The light was with ⟶s, doors open to the street, smoke and feathers.

'The whole scenario, like a Rosicrucian Manifesto, is there in his *Illuminations*. I won't even try to sound it in French. But in aborted English, the elements . . . a few fragments . . . shave it down . . . terrifying . . .

"I responded by snickering at this satanic doctor,
& finished by getting to the window –
Phantoms of future nocturnal luxury

*

We would wander, nourished by the wine of caves &
the biscuit of the road, hard pressed
to find the place & the formula

By the grouping of buildings, in squares,
courtyards & enclosed terraces,
they have ousted the coachman

*

On the slope of the bank, angels fashion their robes
of wool in pastures of steel & emerald . . .
meadows of flame . . . on the left the compost of the ridge
is stamped down by all the murderers . . . all
the disastrous clamours spin their curve

The pivoting of rotting roofs

*

I stepped down into this carriage where period
is adequately indicated by the convex windows,
Bulging panels & contoured seats

The vehicle turns on the grass of an obliterated highway:

& in a blemish at the top of the window on the right
swirl pale lunar figures, leaves, breasts
Unharnessing near a spot of gravel

*

Here will one whistle for the tempest & the sodoms

*

The accidents of scientific magic
The luminous skulls upon pea seedlings

*

The banner of bleeding meat
The moment of the sweating room"

Heat is prophecy.

"Satanic Doctor, window, place. Courtyards, ousted coachman. Left and right. The vehicle, the obliterated highway. Banner of bleeding meat. Moment of the sweating room."

Take this malarial possession and drive it to Africa. Burn it in the furnace like a rotten bandage. Hack it off. Chatterton's Africa, the Eclogues, the imaginary salvation. Tame the river. It's always too late.'

For a moment, of necessity, it died. We swallowed, licked around the rim of our glasses. Then Joblard took it up.

'In Canterbury today, teaching, I heard the fag-end of a lecture on Van Gogh's time in London. Some highly-scented bitch from the Courtauld Institute.

Early 1870s he was here, with a dealer, then teaching, and with some mad job between clergyman and missionary. He had to walk about the East End, *where* I don't know, she wouldn't give you anything specific. Collecting school fees. He also preached a series of sermons. I can see him in the open-air pulpit at Mary Matfellon, spittling the winos, haranguing the derelicts of the future.

They only had one slide to show from this period. It was a sketch he made of a horse-drawn coach, travelling to the left, a swirl of shading in the ground, containing names and signatures; couldn't decipher them. The coach is empty.

I flashed to another, hired, carriage, much later, 1889, driven from the asylum on a farewell visit to a girl in the brothel at Arles, one summer afternoon.'

We pocket a bottle of Armagnac; there is a promise of whisky also – at the studio. The three of us, whistling, through the silent warren to Pear Tree Court.

Joblard's genius is partly expressed in his ability to manipulate the surface of the material world so that, despite all the odds, and while all his peers are going under, he is always supplied with a space in which to work. Dines well, cigars, holidays in villas. Some kind of improbable shape-shifting knack, slipping through periods and disguises, dressed for the abattoir or the tea-dance. Now with a white linen jacket. The castoffs of nautical novelists, backwoods tree-carvers, *Blue Mink* percussionists all fit, as a second skin. He can borrow from Wellesian gourmets or midgets; the garment, once transferred, is immediately his. Nothing looks new, nothing is decayed.

He unlocks the door. A long room under the now pressing sky; a skylight, star-tile in the roof peak. It is another of Joblard's secrets. Like Sickert, he had his bolt-holes. The work, the thing made, was the only reality.

Was that a tenable claim? Not altogether. But as a claim, it stood.

Jack found a chair, his feet upon a roll of opaque plastic sheeting, unplugs the brandy.

Joblard's work is scattered: a pouring of lead; an anvil that might be for use, or might be the work itself; long bow or harpoon on the floor. Elements that could connect, or could be abandoned, broken down, turned into other machines. Bones become lines. Faults run into veins. There are many drawings, star maps, x-rays. A theatre of transformation: surgical rather than gestural.

The generosity of manner ends at the door. Joblard hangs his jacket over a propane cylinder, rolls up his sleeves. If he talks about the work it is in immediate and practical terms. But there is no flannel about craft or technique. He hits you with the basic counters: flayed skin, steel sheet, *folding*; rib, joint, *poured*; parchment, paper, salt. As we look at the objects – he does not speak of them, but of some other thing, some thing they *might* become, or might once have been. His face reflects the potential light of the act implied in the object. Harm is here; is contained. The object is its own defence.

This is the richest moment.

When the total assembly is made, when the action is fully described and named, then part of what is here now is closed off: there is a waxed seal.

We light our sumatras from the gas gun, which is then hooked over a tripod, giving a pale cave light. The mad shadows deform us. We are spread back. The bottle standing on the floor between us.

'I want to remake what has never been made before,' claims Joblard, grinning savage, one chipped tooth, breakfasting on the thunder stone. It is a night of extravagance, linked by the blue fire tongue, the triangle of utter calm.

'The ghosts are more tangible than the human presences, the animated clay dolls. I want to re-enter the familiar and discover its dangers. I will name nothing.'

Jack, the long man, sniffs, something over-ripe, hair standing in clumps, disguised presence, allergic to pretension, breaks in; not interrupting, continuing, taking up the torch, putting his hand to the flame. His tale.

'One January I was working as a decorator in the flat of a Steiner disciple, flower painter, at 16 Chepstow Place, Westbourne Grove. All day off the ground, scratching flakes of ancient paint from the ceiling, eyes sore, dry throat. Handless man. She's out most of the time, getting ready, leaving for Australia, a man.

Comes back late in the afternoon, cup of herbal tea, says, "Oh, by the way, did you know this was the room of the Suicide Club, the actual address?"

It was already a strange time for me. I only took the job to get at her piano. Downstairs was a Radio Times theatrical, Beckett man, his wife, nervous in dark glasses. Dusty glamour of obscure fame. Claims she is writing "metaphysical detective stories". But their main occupation is table-tennis, in the back yard, coats, gloves, mufflers; long ritualised bouts.

The radio was on all day: a comet crashed into the hills behind the cottage where John Cowper Powys lived. I'd just come back from there, mad trip, sponsored by a ragtrade lunatic who thought he was some kind of zen master: meaning that he could hire and fire a dozen tremblers a day, and do Groucho Marx imitations on the telephone. He shipped me to the slate quarries in a red Ferrari to turn *A Glastonbury Romance* into a three-act opera. When I got back – my job was gone and I was done for stealing the car. Shocked into enlightenment!

I'd work into the night: the moon gibbous and threatening. She wants me out, got her yoga routine to complete. I'm getting nowhere, a couple of feet a day. The ceiling's like treacle; no blood in my arms.

And walking back to the underground, all these bandaged patients behind tall windows, convalescent, lobotomised, sitting at individual tables waiting for food, being watched by children's television.

I buy a *Standard* and read of the murder, that morning, in a near-by street, of James Pope Hennessy, the biographer of Queens. He's been stabbed in the head. Died from inhaling his own blood.

When I get home I dig among my Stevensons and discover that

16 Chepstow Place was *not* the address of the Suicide Club, but the address of a Mr Bartholomew (ha!) Malthus, who inhabits that story, suffering a "Melancholy Accident" and falling to his death "over the upper parapet in Trafalgar Square, fracturing his skull and breaking a leg . . . Mr. Malthus, accompanied by a friend, was engaged in looking for a cab . . ."

In November I saw reviewed in *The Sunday Times* the book that Pope Hennessy was working on in his study at the time of that definitive interruption: a biography of Robert Louis Stevenson.

My wages were gone, forty pounds, the precise amount required for membership of the Suicide Club.'

Now the line of new light drives across the floor. The gas tongue so pale its power has gone. The marriage is almost on us. We have slept on our shields. Man to man to man, silent, sunk, the unwilled exchange, the talk brought to its finish. No more to be done, the word is – on.

To the obelisk. Unspoken. It is time to walk, return to the domestic chamber, to Camberwell, to dress the day.

But first we will walk that small mystery, make that connection: from the obelisk of St Luke, Old Street, to the demolished obelisk of St John, Horselydown, by way of the extinguished church of Mary Matfellon, Whitechapel. The three enclosures of ruin. Unacknowledged, but not concealed. St Luke, roofless, wild space in a border of stone; St John, a rim of the original onto which a place of business has been grafted; and Mary Matfellon, nothing, a field with a diagram in the grass, a stain only. The shunned Apostles.

The less they are, the stranger they become.

The walk has nothing to do with lines of force, immaculately ruled patterns, stern geometry of will, pentagrams, grids, brass-rule control. It is older and wilder. The triple spiral, finger print, found at New Grange. The spiral that winds out of Clerkenwell into Whitechapel into Southwark. It is not precise, it can't be measured. But it is invoked. We want it and that is its truth.

The freshness of the day and the obelisk an absolute white, white beyond white, against the dim dirt-grained stone of the body of the church. The fence is breached and the door to the tower unlocked.

This is an act of morning.

We are lifted. The steps in time, wide. Counting the climb as if we would never again descend to the same city.

And raising ourselves by the ascent of this risk. Entering the blade. Beyond the door of light – the skin of the local is shaken. We climb, turning, winding into the tower but, strangely, it becomes a *descent*. We go down towards the sky.

A great bell hangs, a bulk of danger. Old wood. A pillar fallen across two disks or bowls; upturned scales. Spidery darkness. Cool breath. The soupy smell of stone dust, cloth dust, dust dying into dust; ropes on the floor, broken boards. We climb into the dark.

And now Jack is framed across the circular space of the window where the clock once hung. It is the ghost of a rose, unfolding rose of time, twisted into iron: it is a filter, projecting the rose onto the city. Jack's outstretched arms break the circle, Adam Kadmon.

I turn from the light to Joblard. He is leaning back against the skirts of the bell, his breath gone. Out of the heat vortex. His face has died. He is white, bearded in shadows. It is the face of my father. The Father of Lights.

His spine resting on the buried bell. The bell within the obelisk. The cancelled bell that has been hidden from the world.

A flutter of birds against the window. Bird lime. Stench of old feathers.

We turn away, our prayers are made. Down into the face of the lion: Bunhill, Finsbury, Sun, Appold, Pindar, Spital, Steward, White's, Thrawl, Matfellon, the path of old stone: by the

Minories to the Tower, to Horselydown and the Old Kent Road.

To be shaved, washed, suited.

Joblard's room has been cleared of its detritus; the brown swallowed in pale shades, the windows polished, open to the new day. A white cloth spread.

The room-dividing panels have been forced back so that the space is doubled, lit through. Flowers, lace. And by these changes, and on this day, a marriage is made.

18

NOTHING uses me to it.

James Hinton turned heel at Limehouse, would go no further: as if it could be walked out, as if he could unravel the pain, give it a fixed distance and stamp it down. His fists smashed against the iron gates, head bowed to his old enemy, the wind; force gone out of him. The high tower of St Anne's church offered no resistance: it *made* the wind. Hinton obeyed the dead. He was one of them. A sensation not experienced by many mortals – to have no place among the living, to live less than those dead bones, those humps in the ground.

There was a horrible sense of continually walking into himself, falling behind, gone, dead on arrival. Seeing himself, leaning on the gate, a drowned man, the octagonal capped lantern of the tower rising from his head, cuckold, making him an insect. To be blown where the wind chose. The will was gone in him. He would not listen to his own death.

He turned towards annihilation, the labyrinth again, the secret heart. Saviour of women. There was nothing to fear. By passion would passion be killed. Prostitution is dead, I have slain prostitution.

In Church Passage, off Mitre Square, a woman is waiting. Think what a work had to be done! Blessed is he who has found his work! Nothing to be said; she lifts a hand and puts it upon his shoulder. Rust-coloured hair, her eyes have him, brown, wood varnish. He pulls her by the wrist. She drags behind him.

There is no drama, debate, discussion. She was waiting. And

now it is she who is leading him into the narrow gash of Angel Alley. Black straw bonnet, tilted, some fur at her collar, three large metal buttons. Jaunty, a bit of a turn. Name is Kate. Unasked. Name is Conway. Name is Kelly. Tattoo on forearm. Name is Eddowes. Heavy workman's boots, unlaced. Soap in her pocket, ribbons.

Hinton sniffing at her apron: God's instrument. The maul. Within the passage; Hinton under the bell of her skirts, so many skins, so many layers. The print, Michaelmas daisies. Dark green petticoat, stained, not fresh. Hinton presses his face to her belly. She lolls back, complacent, a song from the halls, counting the line of bricks.

Nothing to fear; Hinton has her legs parted and is driving against her, bruising her, she is bumped repeatedly against the wall. He cannot finish it. Not blamed, the woman, for nothing. His arms under her stocking'd thighs; has her lifted from the ground, her boots kicking out. He touches the tip of her womb.

Turns her; now a dog, skirts thrown clear, clutching his fingers into her thighs, sweating, gasping. Rolls off her, still aflame, blood-charged, raw. His pocket-knife; hacks the buttons from her jacket, throws a coin at her feet. Returns. It cannot be drowned. Covered. Crushed. Kept down.

Crosses, through the traffic, the carts and carriages, the people: a wild shadow. He can hear nothing but the dead in their bells. The stones will not hold them. They will grow from the earth. Grave-words: re-sting, not "resting". Hornets.

There is a drinking trough, or shrine, in the wall: the stone moulted, creased, the skin of deformity. A memorial to *one unknown yet well known.* And, through the mouth of this Caliban, a pipe has been driven, a hole. Hinton, on his knees, looks at the stone of sacrifice.

Enters the field of Matfellon, dragging the prostitute, hand in hand, bowed under thunderous clouds, a new Adam and a new Eve.

"'And there was given me a reed like unto a rod: and the angel stood, saying, Rise, and measure the temple of God, and the altar . . .'"

He releases her, unshriven, to climb the ladder into the roadside pulpit: howls.

"'And he had in his right hand seven stars: and out of his mouth went a sharp two-edged sword: and his countenance was as the sun shineth in strength.

Write these things which thou hast seen, and the things which are, and the things which shall be hereafter;

The mystery of the seven stars which thou sawest in my right hand . . ."

It is the time of the ending of time. And a child shall be born, white as the lamb, a saviour will come. But *you*, who are called Sodom and Egypt, are not worthy of the child; you are the dead begetting the dead. And there is no hope for you. You have made my temple a place of shame; it cannot be measured, as your days are measured. Women couple with beasts upon my sacred altar.

And the child that is born shall be an Antichrist, god of unreason, Babylon. You shall follow him in travail, yea, to the end of your days.'

The woman crawls over the field towards a plane tree where another woman and a man are sitting, disputing a bottle. Behind them is the ruin of a defiled sepulchre.

Hinton will confess his penitents. Or flail the skin from their backs. He strides to them, seizing the wrists of the women; he whispers, he spits.

"'And I will give power *unto my two witnesses, and they shall prophesy a thousand two hundred and threescore days, clothed in sackcloth.'"*

The unfortunates drop to their knees under the flaking tree. Hinton is terrible: Mosaic wrath. Old sins nail their palms to the earth. Hinton raves.

"'And the temple of God was opened in heaven, and there was seen

in his temple the ark of his testament: and there were lightnings, and thunderings, and an earthquake, and great hail.'"

But his prophecy is barren; the clouds drift away, to be speared on the towers of another Jerusalem. Hinton, weeping, claws the topsoil, Enkidu, buries the three buttons. Matfellon must be destroyed in fire.

A rim of old Fathers watch him. Stone beards. A spark. The tinder of the organ box.

In one hour the church was gutted. Molten lead poured from the roof. The organ pipes twisted and whistled. Glass burst in the martyred windows. The cracking of saints.

Hinton's boat burnt. An ark of fire.

He dug himself into the grass, to ravish the ground, pain-ecstasy, sacrifice; shivering, gasping; hard clay, the spoiled field bleaching slowly to gold.

On the following morning the watch committee, dignitaries, welfare, the charitable fathers walked over the ruin of Mary Matfellon. Lead in shining pools on the grass. Blood splinters from the windows. Calcined stone. Wood crumbling like skin to the touch.

And in the wreck of the church roof they discover twelve sealed coffins that had been secretly lodged. The coffins were small, a few feet in length, black from the fire, but undamaged.

They gave the order for the seals to be broken: and found within the perfectly preserved bodies of twelve very young children, tightly wrapped, their eyes now closed.

19

DRYFELD LIVED nowhere. He had a room, but could not allow it to be where it was. It was cancelled space. And he was caged in the middle of it. Nobody visited the room, so nothing was added. The blinds were down, the radio was on. He could feel hair, unstoppable, coming out of him; shoving out of his scalp, against gravity. Why wait?

Nicholas Lane lay in the London Hospital in an empty bed; glucose dripping into his veins. The book was so much powder. He might as well snort it. You couldn't kill him, he'd live for ever.

But sometimes, these last days, the world left Dryfeld. He was in it, making for Sidcup, pumping along on the pedals, already calculating how he would sell what he had not yet bought. Then he wasn't. Keeled over at the side of the road, blood on his shirt, a few bruises. Or back to himself with a mile or two missing. There were these gaps in his head. He was spotted with darkness.

Why wait for a spectacular date to kill himself? Why not do it now? Get his retaliation in first. They say that people who talk about suicide never do it. They're wrong.

He found a plastic bag but it wouldn't fit over his head. The bull! Even stretched it looked like a jester's cap, an uncut caul of soapy skin.

He'd studied all the how-to-do-it manuals. So what? The easiest thing was to dive in, get it done. He found another bag, with a book in it, *The Two, the Story of the Original Siamese Twins*. He stopped to flick through the pages, didn't rub out the original price, never bothered, not worth more than a fiver – but the bag was big enough.

Dragged it over his face, which wrinkled, drowning, squeezed in on itself. Bog sacrifice. Eyes hooded over, nose flattened. He didn't even bother to lie down. Took a roll of brown tape and gave himself a collar. Sealed his head into the bag, an unreturnable offering.

Red bands at the border: darkness beyond. His mouth opened. He started to swallow his tongue.

The telephone rang, loud, but far away. Nothing to do with him anymore. It went on ringing. He wasn't going to die to the sound of the telephone. He split the bag across his mouth.

'Yes?'

'Fancy an Indian? There's something coming up, in Boston, I'd like to talk about.'

'Right! Twenty minutes, Brick Lane.'

His face, scarlet, the flaps of the bag hanging like torn ears. No mirror to watch him. Let's go.

20

SUMMONED by telephone, licked in sweat, pale, a kind of recurring occult malaria: I tremble. Make shift through the last traces of the old streets; the hulks are crumbling to dust. We will never get back. The warren is detonated. They disguise it, cover it over with respect, modesty, forward planning: destroy it, utterly. You will never rebuild the city from these words. You would build a monster.

'Bury the beast,' said the girl from Sag Harbor. Her husband had floated it; friend of the trees. Bury Christ Church, Spitalfields, in earth. Incarcerate its hieratic bulk. Lift up a new mountain. To oversee a New Age. Seal its power. Stop its mouth.

Even the brewery is encased, is sheeted in glass, false reflections; disguised with vines and shrubs. The Eagle is hooded. Sell off the portraits.

Bury the bell!

Hold concerts in the belly of the church. Summon the musicians, tame the doctors. Banish the phantoms, the vagrants. Feed them into submission. Bandage the lunatic. Stack cars above the sweating room. Spray it with concrete.

I am shaking, beside myself. Old breath of poison. Flesh of the albatross. Tremor of cold excitement; estranged from any recognition of time and place.

It is a moment of Manichaean necessity – the split one meets, merges, dissolves: reintegrates? On the future's sharpest edge. Holmes and Moriarty plunge together into the torrent, but only Holmes returns, diminished. Without the dark double, the contrary, his own power is lost.

Walking again, turning, it's still the first time, into the Seven Stars.

Who is that sitting in my corner? What's happened to the wall-paper, the ships, castles, the river? A man is waiting for me. My drink is already on the table. I don't need this, I need brandy.

The man is scented with patchouli, his hair, a buoyant ash-grey; it's not Gull, it's not my father. Who is this? He's got earphones, he's connected to a red plastic box. Broad, full-chested. Not one of the workers.

The Brides. The dance of the Pleiades. Not Orion: O'Ryan, the Huntsman. He's transcribing arcs of pure motion. He's smoking. The speed of nerve gives him an amphetamine stutter.

It's Joblard.

And again he has worked a transformation. He has got out of himself, folded back all the inessentials, all the human tentacles, packed them – so that his form is dense. The shell is hard, but more brittle.

Drink runs through the skin of my head, never gets inside me. He calls for more. The glass is taller; I roll it across my brow.

Joblard is making some kind of confession. I can't take it in. Trust is fractured and will have to be remade. He has mutilated the previous, the creature that he has impersonated for so long: by choice become a new man and, yes, there is a new woman.

The orphan is, again, his own father. And because of this is an orphan once more. He is cutting himself loose. Mad with pain. And mad with new pleasures. Unshaven, drinking it, the long weekend.

Unwilling; I am implicated. Soon and sudden. Behind the thin walls, an inhuman voice: 'Don't break the ring!'

"It is remarkable that the skin of the penis and scrotum was perfectly normal in every respect."

Merrick allows the room to perform its cellular function. The long evening slides over his window; brick dust, the shadows of birds. A nurse, crisp scratch of her skirts, pokes at the coals in his grate. The moment holds breath, like a studio oil, darkens into its frame.

His sitting room. A doll's house. Silver tongs. Ornaments, pictures. Volumes in fine bindings; quite a respectable collection. Hair stroked across his wrist, sensitised. No mirror: the doorspace filled, suddenly, by his protector.

"A little excursion."

Curtains shutter low theatre lights that lift the eyebrows. Demonic masks of glittering, scale-like, paint. Hell poses. Slow dancer struggling to lift their dead limbs.

The coach summoned.

Joblard is pursuing the invisible.

'I want to make tracings of unseen acts. To flood locked rooms with chemicals that trap the slightest movements of light. To cover all the marks of my own complicity. I want erasures. Weak illumination of ink. Shaded bulbs hung over parchment. The word "whisper" in some unknown language. I want the acts to repeat. I want to measure the force of decay in bread, the glow in the bones of mackerel. To erase time and to bend its direction of flow.'

I don't know if he is saying this to me, or hearing it on his headset: or if I am making him speak. My fever rubs out the connections. The defences are all down and the shift is on.

I know there is nothing to be written: all writing is rewriting. That old dream: completed books that will never be transcribed, made redundant by their own conception.

The room has filled, but the dance is unbroken. The dancer slips off a black gauze shirt; her body is young, younger than the last time. I can only watch the reflection in the mirror behind her. A shudder of rhythm through her back, slowed convulsion, as she sways her shoulders. She is detached from what she does and detached from her audience. The act is ritualised. Curse and blessing of Enkidu. The pearl. The shed of feathers. She gleams; her hands lifting and covering her breasts.

Now Treves was beginning to take a positive relish in introducing Joseph to new experiences: subtle pleasures could be derived from watching.

Joseph was bathed; fussed over by nurses, tub dragged before the fire, thick warm towels. Treves hovering, always, hand on hip, fingering the links of his watchchain. Escorted into the evening, not knowing if he would ever return: the purpose of his journey a mystery. To make it a routine: that each day should be a rehearsal for the next.

Out on his stick, the coachman's arm about his shoulders; across Bedstead Square, the herb garden, to the street. Lifted into a sealed cab. A flick at the horses. Treves, arms folded, smiling; blocks the window.

Those first autumn evenings: mildness, death. Hay on the pavements. Bales brought on carts to market. Horsedung. Groups in the doorways of public houses. Political meetings.

The route was varied but the duration, seemingly, fixed. No conversation. Tense, rapt. The interval between these excursions was not to be anticipated.

He walked the labyrinth for fifteen years, never encountering the minotaur. The minotaur is outside. We only plunge deeper into our own confusions: turn away and the maze unravels. It is a ghost trap. Walk its length out into the countryside. The path drops through barley fields to Landermere, the estuary. And is repeated in a meander of ditches.

Open the gates of the heart. We force ourselves against the

valve. The seals are there to be broken. Upon the door of a decayed greengrocer's shop, Virginia Road, is painted the map of the labyrinth.

The artist has "gone away", associate of villainy: his grievous body, harmed. His oils dumped among potato sacks. Violent panels. Brawling heads scratched among pint pots. Palette dipped in industrial slurry. He has located the fear and nailed it to his door.

His wife has gone. Tear it down. He is betrayed. The names of birds mark the entrance-gates: from Birdcage to Spread Eagle. Beasts guard the exits: avatars of the Black Bull. Blast them with red light, shatter them in a furnace of sound.

She is twisting, on her back: the floor. As if sacrificed. They close in, tight, to cover her with coins. Naked to the pelt. They are cattled by an ambiguity of need. What is and is not offered.

Joseph's fear was caged. Another time; a fairy tale, a Penny Story. Private box, the nurses in evening gowns, scented, hair dressed; they shade him from the eyes of the curious. Erase his attendance.

He was awed. He was enthralled. The spectacle left him speechless, so that if he was spoken to he took no heed. He often seemed to be panting for breath, thrilled by a vision that was almost beyond contemplation.

As the dancer walks among us the body of Joblard's attention is bound to her, as with a cord. His confession has made necessary some further act. The confession is not singular; it deletes the past, recasting casual acquaintance into a darker intimacy.

She has wrapped a lizardskin coat around her shoulders, naked otherwise, the scorch of the dance contained: perfume, spiked heels. He folds paper into her cup. Gives the word; whispers. I watch the collar of this coat, glittering, in the long mirror. A snake-rope. She will come with us. They are eating Indian.

"My dear, come along, you will be comfortable."

'Shit or bust,' says Joblard, gripping his right forearm with his left hand. On the square. Dynamic tension. And another barley wine.

'All or nothing.'

Now it is random, it is anything. My fever has cooled to a clammy chill, shirt soaked from blue to black. 'Hinton cops out. These restraints. Whips it, fans the fire, then refuses to follow his reasoning to the death. Dementia of the monk, the self-flagellant. Vision of the snail. Unless we can *exactly* repeat the past, we will never make it repent; it will escape us. Nothing is exorcised. It goes on for ever.'

New weather shifts the colour of time. Concentration breaks with close thunder. A torrent. Melting skies. Bones greasy with fright. We run across the Lane. The dancer, squealing, her gleaming skin pulled tight; wobbling on absurd heels.

We are occulted: seeing the future by flashes of lightning, seeing the present from underneath.

Gull redeemed his time. When it was the hour of action, he acted. There were no instructions or whispers from secret masters: no sealed orders. A plot of ground in St Patrick's Cemetery, Leytonstone, was unfulfilled. There were shadows: in the mortuary glass he saw the shape of the burial party. He looked across the estuary and saw the white men rising from the water: the unclaimed dead.

It was the time of the Ghost Dance. Mahdi. Messianic spasms. He saw the verges. John Wilson, Moonhead: God's Son returns to us, coming out from old man Coyote. The trodden circle of the dance. Swallows itself. The dream. He put on a white shirt. The man returns from death, with gifts; towards this city. Heart stopped.

They questioned the Plains Indians that Colonel Cody brought over to the Tenter Ground for his Wild West Show. They were implicated, suspect; sitting on their heels outside the flapping hill of canvas, smoking.

The great synthesis travels in a sealed cab. Stars move across the pitched ceiling. A coracle. They tell of a love that is beyond heat. Jupiter combined with darkness and a piece of the moon.

But ours is the restaurant that is shunned: it is tainted by journalism. Hot lies creep onto the plate. Cockroaches slither down the flock. Let us eat the spiced meats, the saffron rice. Let us take wine. Corrupted music emerges through the distortion of fault as something new.

The girl is persuaded to dance for us, privately; the doors are locked, the shutters drawn.

By carriage across Whitechapel Road and into Brady Street, west, between the Jews' Burial Ground and the Station; skirt the Workhouse; Bakers Row and into Hanbury Street, south now: the moon cuckolded on the great church tower.

In the room Treves holds consultation, mixing authority with humour. Merrick is carried up and placed in a heavily cushioned, rug covered, cane-chair. Treves: his back to the window. The coachman, settled in the frame of the door, ushers in the women: the old one and the girl.

Merrick half-rises; the left hand, gloved, held out. A bubble of address gobs his throat: mucoid leer. Is he here as witness or participant? Oilcloth across the window. Cobbles in the street. Men wrestling over a bottle, a mud dance; keeping it, delicately, between them, keeping their balance; over the kerb, into the gutter. A head wound opens slowly into a mouth: blood-soaked hair. Fire in the market.

Around the brazier, vegetable refuse is burnt; torn with palsied hands, crammed in the mouth. Teeth stumps champing and gumming the shells. Waste-water boiling in the can. The bottle passing between the window and the moon.

"I was awakened by a kitten walking across my neck, and just then I heard screams of murder about two or three times in a female voice."

From above it is a feast: of feathers, wounds, feet on earth. The century snake dying. White clouds boiling slow, a cauliflower scum. Ragstone watching its history evaporate under a gun of steam. The doctor with a womb in his bag. Two men and a woman crossing the Lane towards the lights of a restaurant.

Gloved hand sealing the window. The howl of a dog in an empty courtyard. Her linsey skirt unbells. The banner of bleeding meat. The moment of the sweating room. I heard a voice singing. Widows and unfortunates. No light; all's quiet.

It is *Strange Case of Dr Jekyll & Mr Hyde*, written by Stevenson, after a series of hideous nightmares; received and transmitted by those tuned to accept the scalding stream of images that both mask and reveal his appalling message.

Treves was determined to reverse this process. He had found his Caliban, his Hyde, his natural man: needed now to absorb him, to give fire to his own nature, to the hidden being within – swimming back out of the mirror of deformity into the urbane and politic surgeon. To reclaim the aboriginal, the green; the skin of fruits and scales, the mineral cloak. To manifest his true consciousness. To script that journey within the boundaries of expectation.

When she is naked and glistens, rubbed with oil, garlanded, her skin now darker, they bring out the mask, the great Elephant's Head of Ganesa. So she sways, she lifts her arms, so she rolls the massive helmet of wood. She threatens the moon with her tusk: the tusk that was broken off to take the dictation of the gods. Now it spears Joblard's side.

'Bugger your Sufi dancing – I'll learn the tango!'

We are in an upper room; the moon, the brewery clock, the tower of the church. His face shone. He rubbed down the matted hair of his body, he rubbed himself with oil. He appeared like a bridegroom.

Now the tusked head is on a hook. They are lying upon a couch. The window is the mirror that I block out.

The squatting strangers heat the *ganja*: leading us into a further nightmare.

I felt a cold breath at my ear, and a voice whose inflections were most familiar, although I could not identify its source, said, 'This wretch, who sold his legs for drink, has stolen your head and replaced it, not with an ass's head, but with an elephant's head.'

Utterly bewildered, I went directly to the mirror. I might have been mistaken for a Hindu or a Javanese idol: my brow had risen, my nose, grown to a trunk, drooped to my chest, my ears grazed my shoulders, and to make matters worse, I was indigo, like Shiva, the blue god.

The promise of the Maitreya is here, the coming ancestor, the Buddha of the New Age, the golden one, the Jesus.

On the flame of that promise, they turn and rise. Her shirt is tied around his waist. The shadows of her tassels are skulls. The blessing and the curse. One humped shape shuddering the wall, fading it to glass, letting in the trace of heavenly orbits. He sacrifices himself, leaves himself: the man who emerges from that room is a different man, with larval energies to unleash, furious, but more vulnerable.

The old woman on the bed appears to be eating her way into the other, a witch – Merrick shrinking back – black mouth towards the head of the unborn child. The apprehension and creation of his own deformity; he pushes back into the chair. Treves has shed his coat, sleeves rolled, no water, pulls the old woman by the shoulder and will lift his creature up into her place.

The coachman leading her out into the courtyard. Treves blocking the window, facing the room. The coachman lifting and banging the woman against the wall, repeatedly driving against her; her head almost broken from her neck, shaken loose, a dried-up orange in a torn stocking. Tongue lolling and dribbling. The waters. Dead eyes. Finishing with her, she falls into the doorway of the house: returning to the carriage, seeing to, petting the restless horse.

The room.

Holding Merrick above the body of the girl, so that he stares directly into her face. And sees what Treves cannot see. Whatever else is happening, he is insensible to all motions and urgencies; whatever else is merely automatic, electricity jolted through dead meat. Staring deep into what the surgeon cannot see: whatever is behind him, supporting his weight, supporting him wholly, back to the window, into the tumorous mat of hair and flesh.

And they are all, just then, entirely one being.

book three

JK

21

To: Iain Sinclair Brightlingsea, Essex
July 1979

Dear Iain,

  with your book I assume we're dealing with serious
matters and there aren't that many books out which are
fundamentally serious in that way, certainly back down into
the deeper sources instead of paying out sycophantic glances
to our small audiences in the hope of finding mutual regards.
No: you have committed your full beliefs in what you've
written and you've meant it all. It's that business of *actually*
meaning what's said that I look for.

And first, we find of course a Blakeian stance towards good
and evil: very much a Marriage but not of the Christian-like
entities: more the creativities of the new sciences giving birth
to phantoms more fit for our times. There is an easy (and
wrong) attack on your position at this stage of discussion: it
is that you have involved yourself with a sort of demonology
and that doing so was an emotional error akin to that, say,
of becoming involved with sex magic (and I *am* very hostile
to all magical activities involving power-operations of bad or
twisted feeling). I say that such an attack would be wrong,
though I do acknowledge that to let one's imagination flow
out towards the Bradys or the Krays of the world carries
with it always an implication of at least some prurience (and
prurience *is* a fault). I remember asking you about this in
London once, what you were thinking of, yielding creativity

into bad vortices. And your reply I haven't forgotten: "I don't really know: I just feel I have to trust the process." Your reply of trusting the process almost entirely satisfied me, as indeed it should, and I only added in my own mind the rider that it's the more difficult to trust the process in poetic-heartedness when the role of prurience is there. I think of some of Baudelaire's more dubious moments lifted with such high art into the condition of creative health (*Une Charogne* is one of my touchstones here).

Well, to call your book a dabbling with demons would be to relegate the poetic process to a nothing: I'm only interested in this central question: can the poetry effect the resolution of good and evil into the coincidence of contraries?

We live a news story and enter its present state effected by event and mood: a phantasmic world does arise, *is* appropriate and exact, is even phenomenal for us, rather as a ghost would be. Here, there's a crucial difference between bad poets and good. Any fool can know about these things by reading about them; any fool can construct surrealistic or fantastic visions and, having worked them out, can even see them. But the good poet, working in such fields of knowing, doesn't necessarily "want" to see what he sees; he just sees it, impelled necessarily upon him by circumstance and mood and by his trust in those, his willingness to speak whether gripped by horrors or by beatitudes or by some kind of shining commonsense. I wish I knew what it was exactly that tells us the difference between the man or woman impelled by such necessities to speech and the second-rater impelled by more wary ambitions. But the language has an urgency and somewhat a dread, as has yours here; and there's no mistaking it.

A preliminary positive for me, therefore: I'm not at all sure there wasn't something prurient, wilful, not to say undesirable about certain choices you made before and probably during the writing (why become involved with these matters *before* the poetry began working?); but, once engaged, you evidently saw many things in the phantasmic world, or at least your language came into the light from sources close-bound in that darkness. There is, simply, no mistaking it, as I say.

That is, a phantasm world, with its pairings and opposites, did come "to life" and I mean that well-nigh literally: so we have to live with it.

Let's take the Bradys, though. They have always exemplified for me what I often noted during my own journalism: what appears in headlines as "evil" is also usually banal and depressing.

Your imaginative/poetic vision has called up, summoned, these phantasms, arising from these crimes, but cast them into an astral world where they have another sort of existence. Eliphas Levi was fond of the thought that great evil demands as grand a soul as does great good. I disagree. On the visionary level it is perhaps true because the quality of the vision elevates what it deals with. At certain points of the "dialectic" it is perhaps also true: fear can call for a "grand soul" to overcome it. Also, seen in a vision of a coincidence of contraries, as though succeeding a war in the heavens, it may again seem true. Yet, still I disagree: my own experience of good and evil is that the former ennobles and the latter diminishes the perpetrator in stature. And I put it to myself that the reason is, in a sense, dialectical: in their "fall" from the visionary ontology into the human action it is the nature of evil to limit and depress and disgust – to be small-minded and furious – and it is the nature of good, in its fall, to enlarge and make sunny and bring wider acceptance. Cosmologically, it's the nature of "evil" (now we have to quote it) to be small and furious like an atom-power release, and of good to expand "in love" as the neo-Platonists used to say. We cannot deny the universality of dark/light: our poetics must have that ontology. But we have no referent for value unless our ontology works towards the good – takes that as direction. (And I haven't said yours doesn't, mark you.)

We do need to explore the cosmology on its dark side, to

make our vision unflinching and accurate; so I have no patience with those who, in our own time, would make poetry a bland thing, apparently limited to the pretence of good feeling. But we also need to see that the allure of the cruel is a false allure: that it only holds as grand when seen in its transcendental form (for in transcendence, in their "eternal" phantasm *all* things look grand, good and evil, though our joy and fear tell us so immediately the difference). The more evil becomes precise, *personalised* and located, however, the more it belittles itself: Brady and Hindley listening to those appalling tape recordings (such a *small* bestiality); Gilles de Rais fondling children (such a *stupid* cruelty); a murder case I covered once where a pathetic accused deposed that he stepped into a chamberpot beneath the bed on his way to strangle his mistress; the affinity of the Belsen pictures with the rubbish dump; the cruel schoolboy in Amin or in the Krays; the fact that the schizoid is, in a sense, a *smaller* psyche. All this compared with the grandeur of any small act of kindness in a concentration camp. It is, of course, what Iris Murdoch calls "The Sovereignty of Good", and I believe that the phenomenology, so to speak, of good and evil, in their declension from angel/demon transcendent phantasms, *separates* into the much-in-little and little-in-much. Great evil is a grand conception by our common terms: that is its allure.

In act, it is the implosion into nothing whereas good is the simultaneous fructification of nothing. They are utterly interdependent dynamically and yet good is the sovereign just as "all we have" is sovereign over "all that we shall not have." Unless there is the gradient of value – unless the very coincidence of contraries in the Blakeian sense has itself this gradient, as I think Blake saw – I can explain neither our actions nor our words.

For me, there's another consequence. Out of transcendence what we first create is the phantasm of self, so that we may at all see. I'm hostile to all literatures which, in Foucault-like confidence, think there's a standing from which the self-phantasm can disappear. I can't think of such a standing outside mental illness, and though it's possible to pretend (by various *tricks*) a literature which transcends the question I cannot think it would be curative. That is, the self phantasm must be fully awakened into more universal dynamic but the law is that in all higher awareness the lower forms of awareness persist: they are simultaneously present with the higher awareness. That is why I was so pleased to see in your text this recognition that the self and its phantasmic forms and ghosts must be recognised before the self-as-self-healing or self-"disappearing" can enter the simultaneity of true knowing.

I may have seemed to be writing off the point, but your own kindly dedication to me – "fold the bridge, the cave appears in the middle" – convinces me that I'm very near the point: that your faith remains in the process as curative.

I shall say, therefore, that grand evil is macro-petty because, when we have transcendental visions of it, it scares us stiff into smallness and protection of the self. It is also petty, because, seeing the coincidence of good and evil in the true dynamic, it rejects the coincidence (which is, *I think*, joyful) and chooses instead the obviously worse of the alternatives. Dante is the man who, above all, saw that; Milton wanted to but did not see it. We cannot fail to choose because, short of being gods, we must otherwise vegetate. Only by choosing the good, *because* it is expansive, can we begin to accept the dynamic *in* its duality and yet make a choice. It more truly reflects life process to see that it is creative than that it's destructive at least while time's arrow points in the direction it does and our universe expands: for if evil were sovereign nothing would exist.

Finally, though, I question a sort of sucking-in towards evil in the text: so important to us is that question: how firmly can we build the wall? The truth of such transcendent knowings seems to come into the consciousness of very few (but it is unconsciously known by the many): with all conscious

knowing comes an extra charge of responsibility. By the
gods! we need so hard to trust the process and not ourselves.

Best,
Doug

*

HERE COMES THE FORK, and it is a simple thing to understand – that there can be no mixing of book-buying with the
true work. You can believe it but not, necessarily, be able to
live by it. So that if I am drawn again to Thorpe-le-Soken, I
will stop at the Keep Bookshop, Colchester.

The place has many disadvantages, most of them behind the
counter, but still remains a favourite. It's on a hill, the town
begins here; it's old, leaking, has odd corners – but principally
it has more back rooms, locked drawers, secrets than it has
shelf space. It does the business. The books will come: but you
may not be able to dig them out.

I searched fast, ineffective as a dealer, flinching from the tech-
nical exercise of finding items I could sell; books that were, in
essence, already sold and just waiting to be gathered and
delivered. There are no intrinsic values: absolutely *anything*
becomes valuable if there is a customer for it. That's all you've
got to learn: custodial purchases.

In an upstairs chamber, where psychology shades into per-
version, I found a copy, in well-tanned blue cloth, of *James
Hinton, A Sketch* by Mrs Havelock Ellis; with preface by Havelock Ellis, photogravure frontispiece, seven illustrations; First
Edition, 1918. It was described on the flyleaf as "Scarce", which
justified the asking price of £4. That was too high for me, I
put it back. Who else had ever heard of Hinton? Most people
thought he was his own son. I simply couldn't imagine what had
lifted it out of the £2 class – not, then, making the connection
with that no-man's land where doubtful philosophical effusions
meet with vegetarianism, where theology edges nervously into
sadism: an area that seemed to include Edward Carpenter and
Nietzsche.

I'd made the "accidental" discovery of Hinton in the White-chapel Library one day when the gallery was closed and it was raining. He'd keep.

I turned from the shelf to discover Douglas Oliver, the poet, on his knees, a long black coat, not praying but picking through the Latins. He considers a negotiation for nine or ten volumes, but settles for a drink in the Tudor Room of the Marquis of Granby. A place that needs an intercity train to be re-routed through it.

Of course, I couldn't, or least I didn't, justify my failure to reply to his long and generous letter. I felt that the letter was self-sufficient, its time would come: there was nothing at all I could add to it. If I had in some way provoked the letter – that was enough. I absolutely would not "defend" any position he found that I had occupied. Any kind of "literary" exchange would be doomed before it began. My correspondence had formalised to exchanges of insults on the backs of bills. The nerve-ends that Doug's letter touched are still twitching, and not to be exposed.

This was not the guilt of pursuing a mindless and deranged career, of not opening the writing out, wholly, to the light, shaping it with a precision of trust: what then?

The coincidence of contraries. The meshing and damaging contact of that which is not *quite* the same. The third mind was not present at this meeting. His direction was not to be made clear to me. Nor mine to him.

He was also a disenfranchised Scotsman.

I returned to the bookshop. Bought the Hinton. Walked away up the hill, sun on the stones: old mustard. Day of leaf and bud. I abandoned the other shops and cut directly down into the park beneath the castle.

A ring of children, with watery unlined faces, ran about on the grass, staggering and tumbling. Their keeper was only partly attending to them, listening instead to a history of the walls. The children circled, bumping into each other, their arms out.

One of the girls came over to me, held out her hand, hopeful that I would take her to the swings. There is no fear in these children. They have no shadow of the future to chill their milky eyes. They are without harm.

22

THE LETTER could go no further, *"Dear Hardie"*; his skull resting on his hand like a globe of solid glass. Diffident, unable to make a start: Lees' breath crawled onto the window. He twitched in his clothes. He scratched at his head. He swept aside the blank sheet of paper, took up a book, a paperknife; hacking at the uncut pages.

A line broken by the entry of a court; and just at that point, a certain sinister block building thrust forward its gable onto the street. Audible houses, tenements, vague and sheeted; prolonged and sordid negligence. He was looking at the back of the world. Life was removed.

The awful rushing sensation was on him, getting ahead of event, *knowing*; a dull inevitability. His pride breathes it, lets go, takes it up. Allows the moist heat to form pictures. A woman, churn-shaped; a man, following. The detail floats in from borrowed dreams.

He wipes the glass with the back of his sleeve. Breathes. The picture forms once more.

Suit of scotch tweed, light overcoat, gladstone bag. Crossing towards the lights of a Restaurant. There is a clock on the side of the Blackmail House. A time to be noted. Flare of naphtha. Men drinking.

The howl of a dog. Through the passageway and into the courtyard. He is hard by the door. Knife drawn, a backhanded slash.

It is my duty. The ghost of some old sin, some concealed

disgrace: punishment coming. They are led to the doors of the house. The servants all asleep. No windows. Shriek: *murder!*

So the report is made. What has not been seen is made rational. A time is given to the face of the clock. Lees speaks his fear to authority. The murder is described, taken down, put on file.

The murder occurs and follows his scenario. Is his the only prophecy? There are hundreds; in blood and ink, not codding dear old Boss; typed, pencilled, slated, dribbled over, soaked in semen. Mr Lusk. Everything is foretold. What follows is a pale reflection.

'*That* is the man who cut off her ears!' Robert Lees: pointing from the upper deck of an omnibus at Shepherd's Bush. His wife smiling. 'That is the Ripper, the Harlot Killer.' He is wearing tweeds that belong in a story. He is carrying a light overcoat.

It should be night. It should be another place. There is no blood. Follow the man through the mists. An imposing mansion. There seemed to be some magnetic wave connecting an impalpable sense he possessed with the fugitive. Buckled to the red stuff, t'otherest governor.

But there is no fugitive, no one is accused. An ear in the hand, the prasarved Kidne upon his plate. Drops his fork; I see her face. She is whispering, I cannot tell what she is whispering to me. It is a name at least well known, a name that I cannot mention.

My wife is smiling. 'Robert, the absurdity! You make yourself ridiculous. Following perfectly respectable gentlemen about the West End of London! Dodging among hansom cabs like a street-arab!'

Not Cavendish Square, Brook Street. The Juwes are The men that Will not be Blamed for nothing. Walls, doorways. A plaster rose in relief. You *must* listen to me, Inspector.

I have seen a woman turned inside out. A room decorated with her entrails. The room is scarlet; it is sweating. A woman's voice singing. The smell of violets, left too long in water. They have the talisman. I cannot tell. Carried off or destroyed.

Robert Lees comes up from the Criterion; he had been dining with two Americans. Unconvinced *voyant*, the Inspector dogging his heels; he is barking like a Plains Indian, coyote throat, a time to believe nothing, to cultivate all the fictions. Stamping at the door, his back turned, not looking upon the slaughter, Millers Court, the final act. Demented Lees, responsible, implicated, some magnetic wave connecting him: he leads them, in a seizure – it will make a good story – not directly, circuitously, getting warmer, Boss.

Out from the hot room, the meat oven, to the cancelled spaces. Cooler, much cooler; cold. To Bucks Row, Hanbury, Matfellon, the White Mount, Berners, almost to the river. But it has already happened. He is foaming, white spittle; he is chewing leaves torn from the roadside. He is talking in tongues, prophesying what has already passed. He is seeing nothing. Robert Lees, quite blind, unravels the entrails of the maze. His brain is a stone of coral.

Further out, circling, deeper; it is almost morning. The party arrive at the house of a distinguished public man, at the gates, 74 Brook Street.

Impossible! This man has filled and still fills many of the most honourable offices of his profession, Baronet and Extra-ordinary Physician to the Queen; a philosopher and a man of strong will, yet of gentle presence, with soothing manners and a hawk's eye; one of the most successful of those who have addressed themselves and given their lives to the relief of human suffering and the salvation of human life.

This cannot be, Mr Lees. The physician is not to be lightly disturbed, deflected from his duty; he belongs in the chronicle of society. He has served the highest in the land. Famed for the wise saws of which he is full. He plumes himself on his power of probing the secret hearts of his patients to the lowest depths by eagle glances and by pregnant and pithy pieces of professional sententiousness, enunciated in a melodramatic under-tow. Nothing appears to proceed from the spontaneous emotion of the instant – everything is prearranged. He is a marvellous piece of human machinery.

No, sir. We must proceed with due caution. The doctor is not to be incontinently questioned: there has been a great mistake made. You are ill, Mr Lees. Not yourself, sir.

Persisting, Lees rushes out a description of the hallway: rough porter's chair of black oak, stained glass beyond, a large mastiff at the foot of the stairs. I tell you, it is low-roofed, comfortable, and furnished with costly cabinets, also of oak.

We wait on the servants, until they stir. We are sweat-drenched, dusty, shrunken: unconvinced, on the second step. Ushered directly from door to dining-room. Blackmail House.

The room is long as a street; a girl folding back the shutters. Lady Gull receives them.

'We have, Madame' – Inspector Abberline feels that it is he who is being interviewed, and for the position of bootboy – 'some questions to put to you. There are certain areas upon which you may be able to throw a light.'

The lady of the house, full-figured, easy, adjusts her gown at the throat, turning her face upon her inquisitor, whose back is to the window, red hair on fire.

'Areas? You have ventured out at this inhuman hour to crave instruction – in geography?'

'To relieve us, Madame, of particular difficulties. To furnish us with answers to the questions with which I am obliged, reluctantly, to confront you.'

Her gown, again, tightened. Abberline having an almost irresistible urge to check upon his own potential state of undress; feels that his choice of undershirt is being ruthlessly scrutinised.

'Could we enquire if your husband, Sir William Withey Gull, was at home last evening, at midnight, and for the succeeding two or three hours?'

'At home?' Her voice was low, almost melodramatic.

'Yes, Madame, at home. With you. Here.'

'Do you seriously expect to establish, Inspector, whether *at midnight* my husband was honouring me with his company within his own house? Would you perhaps like to discover how *precisely* he was employed at that hour?'

Abberline finds it impossible to look directly at the woman. And though her hands are heavily ring'd, they are powerful; her face is powdered, her lips savage, her eyebrows quite alarming. He thinks of an owl: feathered immobile calm, razor claws hidden beneath a Japanese wrapper.

'Perhaps, Inspector, it would soothe you to examine Sir William's – bedroom? Are you searching for stolen silver, jewels, furs? You think this a likely crib? I could make arrangements for you to crawl beneath the bed. I will have cupboards emptied at your command.'

'We are here in connection with a peculiarly savage murder. An unfortunate was mutilated last night in Whitechapel. Her womb torn out; her internal organs draped like bunting around the chamber.'

He had gone too far. It was unforgivable. His career was now over. The Lodge was closed to him.

Lady Gull did not shrink from the intrusion of horror. She toyed with a fork.

'You come into my house and you bring with you unspeakable crimes. Crimes that you have now taken upon yourself to articulate, sparing none of the details that would shame a coroner's court. You are quite mad, sir! This *cannot* go unremarked. I shall have occasion to speak with Sir Charles Warren. This is intolerable. An assault! Unwashed from the most barbarous slums in Europe, rubbing against vermin-infested walls, your arms scarlet with blood and filth – to be received in my husband's house!'

A groan from Lees, head in hands. He is once more under the Royal Arch, nineteen years old, demonstrating clairvoyant tricks for the marble queen. Abberline, white to the temples, now doomed, and with a condemned man's swagger.

'If you would allow me, Madame, to examine Sir William's wardrobe our work would be done.'

They climbed the stairs in silence. The Inspector nervously looking out the great mastiff, who was not to be seen.

The bedroom was immaculate. Fresh linen, bright rugs. An undistinguished watercolour, Thames barges. The boots in the wardrobe all shone accusingly. The long coats gleamed, a headless commission of enquiry. Shirts crisp as tissue paper. Forensic collars. Studs. Cuffs.

'Would you care to take away for examination,' said Lady Gull, who remained in the doorway, 'Sir William's underclothing?'

They left, were shown out, deposited in the sunshine. All against the tide of deliveries. Pitched out like dirty milkbottles. Parting, abruptly: the Inspector striding off, to no purpose, with his profession's long experience of making that state look purposeful. On this ability his career had been built. To go by the book when the book said nothing.

Lees was deserted: his visions annulled. They could be transcribed as fiction. The myth, being freed from event, could gather far greater conviction. Released from himself, he hailed a cab; self-indulgent, and hungry, returned to the letter that he could now begin.

Lady Gull walked into her bathroom, sat in a wicker chair to unroll pink stockings, dainty slippers; to drape her patterned robe over a chairback, to face the mirror; full-chested, matted with body hair, right hand upon belly. Her hair was left upon a hook, a hollow cat. The pouting sardonic lips, a little too bright, parted to reveal strong square teeth. The powdered cheek clotted in the steam.

Wiping the mirror with a firm forearm, looks at herself, thick but unaroused, a knotted rope-end. Flattened nipples painted around with star-shapes, mapped skin: Sir William Withey Gull.

23

To: Caroline Haddon "Waiting for a Train", Berwick Station
May 1875

Dear Carrie,

Since our talk together I have wanted to write to you on one or two points. One thing is instructive to me, as to the way in which it happens that my processes of thought seem to me to excite a mistrust or feeling of inaccuracy or partialness, even (excuse me – I only say *seem*) in persons who so appreciate me, and enter into the results of my thinking as you do.

It is what I can scarcely now help calling my fluxion method of thinking; that is, the plan which I am quite conscious of when I look into the workings of my mind, of laying aside part of the visible elements of a case, in order better to see the others. What makes this process right is, that laying aside is *remembered*; and what makes it necessary is the complexity of facts, the presence in all of them, not only of many, but of counteracting or *balancing* elements, so that the results look simpler than they are, and the full extent of some of the things present, can be perceived only by getting rid, in thought, of the mixed-up influences of the others.

I could refer to this process as the *erasure* of the inessential; but I could go further, leap beyond, it does come on me, that it is the obvious and the most apparent that is *not* to be stated. That which is present before our eyes needs no elaboration. It is the invisible that moves us. We arrive at the essence by describing that which surrounds it. To describe the invisible itself would be to erase its power over us. If I listed all the forces that were around me, the rights, passions, feelings, influences – I say, *all* – I would make my own presence wholly unnecessary. By ceasing to be I would however be more powerfully and truly present than I had ever been before. I would be disencumbered, no longer prey to the physical laws of the universe and the grinding tyranny of time. I should never again be before your eyes, a succession of negatives and qualifications, I should be within you, around you, beyond you. In erasing myself I should truly become.

So you see there is a compulsion on me, a necessity – the universal compulsion and necessity by which I believe all deeper seeing has come – to see human life differently, if I am to see it at all. That which is visible in it – is not it. I must see more if I am to *feel* I see it. I must see some hidden things that seem not there at all, but are there, though I will *never* see them.

Now, the fact that has arrested me in social life – perhaps it is emphatically in modern social life, though perhaps not – is the discord between people and what they do; how such people can do such things. This is the problem. What I am perhaps more conscious of than most, is the evil of this good life. And this is, I suppose, the happy fruit of my sojourn in Whitechapel in my youth.

I discovered then that there was a force that operates upon us, a force that our deeds can never describe; perhaps our deeds even deflect that force from its purpose. What is that purpose? It is not to be spoken of – other than by stating: it is that which we choose to leave out. We are now far beyond all notions of good and evil, all merely human morality. This new Heaven is not for greenhouses and carriages. There are no high walls around it. We have prepared ourselves for another "invisible life" but that world has slipped away. When we have surrounded it – then it is gone. And we are the shape of that absence.

Dear Carrie, it is assuredly true that some men and some women will be alive and remain to the coming of the Lord; the very last epoch of human life will be witnessed by some eyes and hailed, or wailed (most likely at first) by some hearts incredulous and incapable of believing that they can be the witnesses of the last stage, the triumph. Then assuredly, too, the last stage before the last stage will be witnessed by some eyes, and trembled at, and mourned over, and disbelieved by some weak and troubled minds. Why should they not be yours and mine?

Your loving brother,
James

St Michael's, The Azores
November 1875

My dear Son,
    Not Corvo, nor Flores. Not Pico. It is at St Michael's, almost beyond the pull of Europe, those tired bones, the dust of its sad history, that I have at last settled. Not at rest, halted. The New World is a rumour across the cold ocean. I cannot hear the fall of those bright feathers, the tooth of the jaguar breaking upon black stone.

I watch the sun die and feel that it is my own brain burning, liquefying, melting, cooling to lead. Patches shine like silver. But they do not remain.

A TRIBUTE

We have heard recently, from Ponta Delgada on the island of St Michael's in the Azores, of the death of the philosopher and surgeon, James Hinton. Acute inflammation of the brain declared itself, and after a few days of intense suffering, in which he knew no one, he entered into his rest on the 16th December 1875.

It would be a pain to me that any Memoir of James Hinton should go forth without a word of affectionate regard for his memory from me. It is now near twenty years ago that our acquaintance began. Sympathies in common on the

The fire in my skull is out. I can watch most calmly as my brain falls out of the heavens, so abruptly, into the great dead sea.

This is where I have come because this is nowhere. Dust. The dust that man is, blowing, blowing. On our lips and in our fingers. The orange groves! All those sad lives; those candles, folded into bulbs of wax. They hang. But they are green, Howard. There is no fire of truth in them. I will not suck on that green blood.

Our dwelling is a ruin, nowhere better. The shutters cannot hold out the dust. I take it on my spoon.

A little girl of ten came to me while I was sitting on the harbour wall and said, 'Do tell me about the fluxions.'

I replied at once, 'Multiply me 17 by 3. So you know 3 times 7 is 21, 1 and carry 2; 3 times 1 is 3 and 2 is 5 equals 51.'

'Now,' I said, 'do you see what you have done with that 2? You have put it down and then rubbed it out; it was necessary to have it, but not nearest subjects of human interest brought us much together. I recall vividly the earnest manner with which he would submit to me his new works, chapter by chapter. Convinced as he was that the only deadness in nature, the only negative condition, was man's selfishness, his whole life and thought was to excite a reaction against it.

Death to him was a purely human idea. All nature is living. He was abreast of the best physiology of the time, and may be considered as having done good service in combating the narrow views that still prevail, even in high quarters, and which would raise a barrier in nature between organic and inorganic where none exists.

Hinton was not a man of science, but a philosopher. Science was to him the servant of philosophy. He felt himself to be an interpreter of nature; not in the Baconian sense by the collection and arrangement of facts, the sequences of causes and effects, but, like the Hebrew seer of old, penetrating through appearances to their central cause.

to keep it. Now, a fluxion is this; it is a thing we need to have, but are not intended to hold; a thing we rightly make, but in order to unmake.'

The world is so beautiful I don't know what to do; the condition of that joy is consenting to bear pain; and one scarcely dares to say one is happy, because it makes the pain confront one, and the words have lost their meaning ere they have passed one's lips.

I am happy and sorry; and just now I cannot see a bit whether that gladness I think is coming on the earth is coming or not.

I am not sure I shall be in a great hurry to come back. There is no reason to move from where I am now. Not even an eyelid, or tongue over dried lips. Why should I disturb the pain that is the only truth?

It is so sad to me that I have lost the power of helping those who need worldly aid. I have tried too much, and failed; but yet perhaps in that, my failure, God is giving me more than I tried for.

I remember one occasion when he came to me full of emotion, with tears in his eyes, at a glimpse he had caught of the universal relation of things to the Divine Cause. 'What I see in nature,' he said, 'is the Divine power acting within an imposed limit. God, self-limited, is the universe. God is not the universe, but it flows from Him and becomes phenomenal by the laws of limitation.'

I could not at the time but check him by quoting Goethe – laying severe stress upon hope, and urging on him that the poet did not seem to admit the likelihood that we should ever realise it by seeking truth as it is. Hinton would not, however, be brought back to our everyday views and imperfect ways of thinking, but insisted that we voluntarily hindered our vision by the mere scientific relation of facts as opposed to a true philosophy of them.

Suppression and reappearance in a new and higher form was to him the fundamental law of physiology. Organisms in upward order, concoct, digest, assimilate, "and corporeal to incorporeal turn."

But, Howard, there is a wrong, an intense wrong, in our society running all through our life, and it will be made righter some day. I dashed myself against it; but it is not one man's strength that can move it. It was too much for my brain; but it is by the failure of some that others succeed, and through my very foolishness perhaps, there shall come a better success to others, perhaps more than any cleverness or wisdom of mine could have wrought. And I hope I have learnt, too, to be wiser. We have not come to the end; though I am so exhausted, that I seem scarcely able to believe in anything before me.

I cover my eyes from the sun but my hands can no longer keep out the light. I can see through! Skin is glass. There is nothing. The darkness turns, turns, an eye on a pencil. It turns faster. And faster. I do not think now that it will ever stop.

your loving father,
James Hinton

Hinton's thoughts on moral subjects were of the same character as those on material. The miserable, despised, and abandoned outcasts of society, sacrificed to the selfishness of the well-to-do and respectable, was a glaring instance of the deception of the phenomenal. I think I am justified in saying, from my first intercourse with him, that he thought such facts illustrated the object of Christ's work on earth, as showing us how contrary truth is to appearance.

To descend to lower matters, I may say that Hinton's physical energy always seemed to me as great and indomitable as that of his mind. Together they afforded an example of intellectual and bodily activity rarely surpassed. The work he did was well done, and by it he laid stepping-stones for others to advance upon.

Hinton's life was not so full of incident as it was full of thought. He was one of the pioneers of humanity through the obscure and dark ways of the senses to the region of truth.

W. W. Gull

24

IAN ASKEAD took us down to look into the fridges. He was a night porter at the Metropolitan, his fawn overall buttonless with rolled-up sleeves; wet-haired, constructing a smoke in his glass cubby-hole – the grim building itself frozen into a kind of malign silence. A mausoleum of impacted wasp-blocks.

We were nervous, oppressed by the locale, which gave him a status he did not have on the street. He had that benevolent Glaswegian charm that goes all the way through mania into self-annihilation. And he did it with a grin. There was an innocence here that would have fed the gas ovens. As victim or as operative. Just as it fell out.

It had been a quiet weekend and most of the fridges were empty. He found one that was tenanted and slid out the white bundle on its tray for our examination. A swaddled something, emitting traces of blue light. In a plastic bag like a Sainsbury's chicken.

Askead, amused by our interest, produces the instruments of pathology, the saws, calipers, head-sets. He plugged in an electric-kettle.

On this stone slab with its sluices at the corners, like a slate billiard-table, the soul is cut free. The bird is sprung. Within this ring of false illumination and under this taint there is a bruised initiation. The conversations of the Indian doctors, the Irish students, are set into the greasy walls; uneradicated. As the skull splits, the words enter. As poison.

It is agreed. We will go with Askead to meet the Victor Haldin Death Cadre, an unlocated splinter of the Angry Brigade, meditating action.

*

Askead, then, sitting in what remains of his underpants, tactically black, on the edge of his mattress, his son, robust and nordic, like the product of an Aryan babyfarm, hands on bars of cot, pisses out a curve of clear gold water onto the matting. New morning. Askead lights the stub of last night's cigarette.

As with old dopers, it's difficult to get him *moving*. Our brief is insecure; we are potential film-makers, lacking only cameras and film-stock. We are invited neither to participate nor to witness. And Askead is only in this for the ruck. Theoretical Anarchy holds no charms for him. A good night out is going over Kilburn to trade insults in the Shamrock Lounge and wake up bleeding on alien pavements. On very good nights he wakes up authentically paralysed in the gutter. And comes home free in an ambulance.

One great night he will wake up in his own fridge.

His wife, who has some kind of position in the household, as child-minder, winning them the use of the basement, is "involved" with a minor technocrat who dresses in Burton's leisurewear. This pleases Askead – who sees it as a context for violence.

'You're a slimy little globe of damaged frog crap,' he spits, gleefully, on sight of the lover, tearing all the buttons from his shirt, before his wife fells him with a cast-iron saucepan. Strong skulled, chipped, not shattered: not even a headache in the morning. The lover goes off to the office, his shirt-front held together with large pink nappy pins.

*

Stoke Newington is the neck of a killing bottle, wearing its

181

entropy without guilt. Cinema-mosques disappearing under a generation of papers, groups, dates, meetings.

Brilliant brickwork of the blacks beating against the shaded Hassidic fringe. Scufflers working the gaps: a gentility that will bring it all down. Everything centred on the police barracks and its boastful spread of wanted posters.

At Abney Park we turn away, break from the pastiched New Kingdom glamour, into a wide leafy avenue. They are waiting, behind the curtains of an upper room.

Multiple locks and chains: everything but a password.

They've got the bottles, but not the petrol. Threats and hand-books and the insides of alarm-clocks. Present anger focuses on Redhill. Barbed wire squat. Neo-fascist bootboys licensed to poleaxe, to sledgehammer, to evacuate. The wolf is at the door. They persuade with crowbars, rip out the plumbing. And this rhetoric is countered by fire-buckets, ball-bearings, paint pots. It is a frontier zone of demented doctrine. Every-thing's boiling but the recipe's been lost.

Denis is savagely bearded in a style that owes something to the cover of the Pan Books edition of *The Dharma Bums*. He wears a black vest, takes up threatening martial arts poses, moving sharply backwards and forwards across the window, compulsively checking out the empty street. His wife, Pearl, is, of course, pregnant again. And the credit for this seems to be awarded to Denis alone.

'Hit back! Situation. Forced. They. Them. Those. Got to watch out. No room. Manoeuvre. Context. Precipitate action. BURN!'

Pearl is doing her breathing. Askead puts his son down among the bottles and looks for one with something in it. He's un-lucky. The room is, in fact, obsessively clean. And could, under other circumstances, be accused of complacent and trivialising petty bourgeois tendencies. Flowered cushions. And a hint of south-coast cargo culting. The coffee mugs are polished. And they have names on them!

Nothing can be done until the contact arrives. We remain

under suspicion. Denis works out with a squash-ball in his fist, as if squeezing the nuts of the Rt Hon (Leonard) Robert Carr.

'Nowhere to turn. Can't let them impose. Conspiracy state. Planted! Trapped. Watched. No room. Landlord. FIRE BOMB!'

The shutter stops-down to a benevolent twilight, but the windows cannot be opened. The phone cannot be touched. *They* are listening, they hear what we whisper. So we wait. Denis counting as he gives Pearl's thigh a chinese burn and she breathes at the second level.

We hear the taxi pull up, the slow heart of its motor. Denis tries to fit a kitchen-knife into the pocket of his jeans. There is some dispute over the fare, points of order to be made. In a guttural Bronx accent. Mixed expletives.

The Invisible Insurrection is postponed. It is the contact.

Skulking into the room with dark glasses and a brief-case, long coat, an abortionist's runner. No names are given, that's understood. Breathing like he's got a slow puncture: the contact is unabashed.

'Hi; I'm Mossy Noonmann. Anyone wanta score?'

*

In this endless night only the locations change. A low-ceilinged basement now in Petherton Road. It's hot, uncomfortable, hands around knees, bundles of laundry.

The dialectic falters. The wrongs can be catalogued interminably, but the action remains opaque.

The meeting had been going since the middle of the afternoon. Dryfeld, in an earlier incarnation, under another name, you can try to identify him in Richard Neville's *Playpower*, was present; but he'd quit, early, deciding to form a one-man splinter group, a new form of Anarchy, by inventing a scam that would rip-off enough loot from the Post Office to get him to America.

Noonmann sidles along the fringes with his salesman's briefcase. His credentials are excellent: he's been thrown out of America and half of Europe, he's borrowed money, he's lied, stolen, cheated and escaped with no moral convictions. The only law is survival. And he's not wholly convinced that he'll obey that. The afterlife of Lazarus, half decayed. I'll stand in the shit if you let me stand on your shoulders. Worthy of Dante.

It is a Dutchman who kicks aside the torpid rhetoric of the merely disappointed. He spins off a dozen ploys in as many minutes.

'You want somewhere to sleep? Go sleep on the steps of the Town Hall. Ok? You camp in London Fields. What's the problem? Do it. Just do it. Let them worry. Use the guilt. The only law is what works.'

As I have the use of a car, I'm the one to drive him. It's my part of town, but he directs me. The man is solid, older than the others. He's bearded, is he? The face won't stick. You can't describe it; it's gone. A beret? Sometimes. Or was it a grey trilby?

I don't know how we got there, I'm listening to him talk.

'They won't do anything. I give them a few pokes but nothing comes of it. Ok? It's already finished, I think.

In ten years half of these will be begging for jobs in the local government and the other half will be junkies. Or both. Ok?'

We park and he leads us down a narrow alleyway. I look at the name in the brick, Angel Alley. It's Whitechapel. It is alongside the Whitechapel Gallery but I've never really noticed it before, one of those slender secrets.

In a room on the left, off the courtyard, there are people standing around a table. They are being given cups of soup and rounds of bread. An oil lamp. Long-headed shadows. They sign a book, pay nothing. Are fed. No questions, no psalms.

On the other side of the court there is a glow from the top-floor windows.

'Come,' said the Dutchman, 'see it.'

Up the stone steps, a long warehouse floor. Dozens of sleeping figures, shapes in bags. So many? Candles at the windows.

'It's easy,' said the Dutchman, 'it's nothing. When you can – you do it. When you can't – move on. Ok?'

*

This is the room. The windows now are filthy, smeared, webbed over. The city is industrial again. Thudding of elephant generators: prophetic smoke. The Masque of Anarchy is cancelled. The dust on the floor is undisturbed. The season has shifted to chill. Joblard is to stage a performance, a Chemical Theatre, an Act of Initiation.

We walk through the locked Gallery; the raven is on the north wall, the owl, the skull of a sheep. The shields, maps, drawings, the burnt wood. We are alone in the building. And a voice. *'Don't break the ring!'* Disembodied, behind us, uninflected. Bare walls, polished floors. Once only.

As the scalp pricks, the phone at the front-desk cuts through with its immediate and insistent hysteria. A friend, urgently, for Joblard. He must get hold of today's SUN.

There's a vendor at the underground entrance. Centre spread: Friday, March 8, 1974. 'HORROR' FIND IN DEATH CASE.

A man accused of murdering his wayward wife had a book which made 'appalling' references to Moors murderers Ian Brady and Myra Hindley, a jury heard yesterday.

The book, by 'performance-artist' S. L. Joblard, called Necropathia, dealt with dead things, said Mr Gilbert Gray, QC, prosecuting at Leeds Crown Court. "There were pictures of bodies, naked and bound, and references in the most appalling print," he said.

The book was found by police at the home of Gilbert Friend, who denies murdering his attractive wife, Pat.

Mr Gray claimed that Friend, a labourer, strangled his wife with a blouse and electric flex after discovering she had made love with a neighbour in his Dormobile.

It is alleged that Friend hid the body in a cupboard at her mother's home and later telephoned his own mother asking her to tell the police where to find the body. He also wrote an alleged confession to his mother. It read. "She wanted sex so she took it. I want her and now I have got her. No one else can have her now.

She asked for a last kiss, but I couldn't.

She raised her face to me and we kissed. I put my hands on her throat. As she died I said, 'I love you.' I am sorry, mother. I love you. I am going now to wait for the end, maybe I will meet her there."

The trial continues today.

Evening. The room above the courtyard.

Not the thing itself but its receptacle. The shadow preceding its source. Dark sentences. The true performance occurs when the audience has left. Wax moulded around electric lightbulbs drips slowly onto the open books, erasing and patterning the text.

From the rooftops the shadows move into cimmerian windows. Now the red is gone: the tincture of mercury. It is the escape of dead light. An act of blindness, hooded figures between lines of repressed fire. The supplicant has heard the question, but no answer is expected. He passes, without lifting his eyes, along the walls; his stick drags in the dust. Gradually, his acts cancel the text. The performance absorbs all of its own potential, folds back in on itself. Nothing is written, everything repeats. Whispering the future down gummed tubes of hide. The voice is the throat.

Joblard's hesitation shudders breath. The ghost escapes. A singe of wax. Memory leaking, unconnected to any past. The empty room. Candle-flames leaving black ferns on the glass. The performance is what happens afterwards. The cup of soft wax takes the print of an unknown key.

But squatting in a corner, they have all gone, is an American girl, with cropped hair and set jaw, resolved, her own game. Intoning the list, playing back the names of victims and variants, within the range of an identified threat; her own compilation, set against the slow ceremony. Nobody listens. Recording a loop, followed by an immediate chorus; her own voice, unrecognised, as it moves, imperceptibly ahead, as it leads her into what she does not know.

Victims and variants, murdering martyrs.

A tide of ash-textured light climbs against the custodial windows. Her head sunk onto her knees. The tape-recorder, an alien presence, detaches itself from her dim intention. The names have escaped. They tremble and manifest in the dawn air, lifted, a shield raised, not in protection, but to strike, the blue signature of a guillotine.

J

ohn Kennedy
ack Kerouac
ohn Knox
ack Ketch

K. Stephen
K. Huysmans

ekyll the Doctor

ubela Jubelo Jubelum

upiter

K

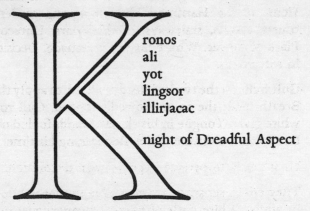

ronos
ali
yot
lingsor
illirjacac

night of Dreadful Aspect

The Coming K
    The K in Philip Dick
  Joseph K

MISTAH KURTZ

Captain Jack is dead – is dead

James Kelly, James Kelly – dead

JUDAS KRISTUS!

25

THE BARE CHAMBER; a half-circle of smoothed stones around a long table. The table is stone also, is pure white. A cut cube. One man, ash-haired, dressed in black, at the head of the corner. The light from the dome is circumspect, veiled. House of the Hammer. Hidden among gardens, fountains, courts, rooms, stairways, double-doors. Unrecorded secrets. Place of power. Where history is remade. Decisions are taken in soft voices.

Gull waits on the twelve. Ready, willed, to apply the compasses. Breath held; the room slowed, stopped. Gull rolls his eye to white glaze. Tongue in his throat. Hands folded over the belly. Dropping the temperature. Redeeming his time.

He is ready to preside over his own dissolution.

They enter, separate, from twelve unmarked doors. Hooded. In white. White gulls of heresy. Incongruous cowls over uniforms of anonymous power; greys, chalks, lime. The instruments are set upon the surface of the table.

'I am glad you were able to come to this place,' Gull begins, 'you necessary twelve. And now the game is on. Twelve London physicals with not a name between them to call their own.'

'Sir William, I am Howard. Dr Howard. The names of my colleagues . . .'

'Are of no account whatsoever, Doctor. Doctor *Benjamin* Howard.'

Gull drew a bag from his pocket and reached deep down into it. 'Would you care for a grape?'

He cut off a bunch, selecting a prime specimen, which he proceeded to rapidly skin.

'Or would you prefer the relic?' He poked the crumpled purple scrap across the table. 'Does it not resemble the foreskin of our Lord? The first drop of His Blood that was shed. Practical people, the Jews.'

He swallowed. 'I take but little wine, but the sugar of the grape seems to supply the readiest refreshing material of which I have in my own person any experience. Grapes and raisins and water, gentlemen. And with each grape a lesson in theology. From the first drop to the glorious conceit of transubstantiation. This is my blood of the new testament, which is shed for many. But which of you will betray me?

You are writing very busily, gentlemen. Putting down your names for fear that you forget them before the end. Do not stop. Write *that* down. And that. And that. It exercises the fingers most usefully.'

Dr Howard drew the white bag from his head. A young man with heavily oiled and carefully arranged hair, thin on the scalp. Simous nose, snuffling, probably with some allergy; rasping.

'Do you want to look at this paper, Sir William? There is nothing written, I do assure you, on its outside.'

He slid the top sheet towards Gull. Who did not move. 'Is the nothing in your own hand, Dr Howard?'

'There *is* nothing, Sir William. Nothing at all.'

'Then it is a forgery!'

'Not of my making.'

'*That*, sir, is my proof. Who said I could not swim?'

The eleven, the hooded ones, scribble furiously over their papers. A team scoring the scorer.

'Sir William, your record and your achievements, recent as well as over the past forty years, are too well known to need my advocacy – but we are gathered in this chamber today in the character of a court of medical enquiry; there are matters, at present wholly in shadow, that must be brought into the light.'

'*De Lunatico Inquirendo*. You are a commission in lunacy. You prove your own fitness to sit upon this commission by demonstrating my insanity. Excellent! I have a Gold Medal in Lunacy; I am Lecturer in Lunacy; Fullerian Professor in Lunacy; Fellow of the Royal College of Lunatics; Resident Madman to Guy's Hospital; Baronet and Mooncalf Extraordinary to Her Majesty the Queen. I rave in my chains; I rattle. The marble is winning, gentlemen.

I have been mad for a long time, in a dream of men, of duties. What doth the Lord require of thee, but to do justly? He requires much more. He requires the truth. I saw more clearly than others. I held that our science alone is sufficient to raise, and will in course of time raise, the human tribe towards a higher form. I believed in a physiological physic founded upon a study of individual peculiarities, and sought not to battle violently with disease but to harness nature's own healing powers. Discover the essence and distil it! I knew power and felt that it was my own. Mad! Mad then. With never a yelp. I sought to become what I was.'

Gull stood up, walked around the table. Dr Howard rose, hesitantly. To confront the outstretched little finger of Gull's right hand, which was intimately threatening his outraged nostril.

'With this humble digit I probed the rectum of his Royal Highness, the Prince of Wales. You notice the length of my first joint? There was only a slight puckering on the anterior wall of the stomach, but his annular structure was so tight that it admitted only the tip of my little finger. The first joint. What do you think, Doctor – that I have not washed it from that day? I have entered the divinity of kings to the length of my finger nail. How many men can say as much?'

The scratching of pen-nibs on paper had altogether ceased. Gull resumed his seat.

'A measure of wheat for a penny, and three measures of barley for a penny; and *see* thou hurt not the oil and wine!'

Gull's broad hand on the table-top. They stare in heat, scorching a print of its outline into the marble. Fingers hooked once more into his waistcoat. Another naked grape, obscenely squelched.

'Observe the dyer's hand!'

Gull placed his right hand upon his left breast with the thumb squared upwards. He bowed with mocking piety.

'Sir William, there is the question of experimentation upon animals.'

'Never harken to a crow that lies, or a dog that tells the truth!'

'You attempted to defend, I believe, Claude Bernard who invented a stove which enabled him to watch the process of baking dogs alive. You justified this hideous performance by claiming, and I quote, "our moral susceptibilities ought to be bribed and silenced by our selfish gains." Of what would those gains consist? *Precisely?*'

'Better prepared meat! I am not a red indian savage. I will not devour raw flesh. If I have practised the necessity of vivisecting animals I have not hesitated to also experiment upon myself. I have watched myself bake in far more fierce ovens. I have seen my fur crisp, my skin crack, my brain burst. And I have had the self-knowledge of what that suffering would mean. I always knew before I began. *That* is exquisite torment.'

'In 1873 you read a paper before the Clinical Society of London, "On a Cretinoid State supervening in Adult Life in Women." It was a justly celebrated account of myxoedema based upon five cases, women from a small privately-funded asylum, under your personal supervision, as part of Guy's Hospital. In this paper you mention nothing of the thyroid gland and of any experiments in its removal. And yet we have sworn evidence that in pursuit of your own wholly unproven thesis you removed these glands, first from monkeys and later from the women themselves; you succeeded in producing a chronic myxoedema, a cretinoid state, with the tissue-changes, physical and mental hebetude, memory loss, the alteration in excretions, temperature, and voice. But, by as late as 1888, no practical use has been made of these barbarously achieved results.'

'If my description of this condition, which ran to no more than five pages, had sufficient elegance and was correctly formed and argued then the experiments that followed were unnecessary, yes. But they were carried through to *cancel* what I had written. I was by that time exclusively involved with uninventing my own history. The traces of acts are cruder than the traces of concepts. I left five cretins to live at my charge, freely and without harm, instead of leaving alive *the possibility* of my theoretical proposals being acted on by five and twenty bunglers, who could not open a laundry bag between them with their scalpels.

I would leave a city of female cretins if I could absolutely erase the work that I have done. Ignorance is the only safety. I have done what was required of me. I say again that I have redeemed my time. I did not fulfil this commission merely to cancel some irritation or threat to those in power, on whose power we all depend. I aborted that insult – but it was of no importance. I acted out the description of an act that was always there. And in doing this I erased it. I freed that space. It could not be left to madmen, prophets, millennial tremblers.

I have hacked out an infected womb that would have bred monsters. But my acts failed. I did not see that they would *themselves* form the shape of a new myth, and that in removing the outline of the old fear I was planting a spoor of heat that would itself need to be brought to earth, chilled to immobility, stopped. The myth kills the myth; makes new, infinite rings, smoke above the white stones. I would unhinge the cap of my skull and let the stars pull wires from my brain. This is a terrible matter. Doctors, *wake up!*'

He spoke with his back to them, but it did not signify. The light was gone from him. A froth remained; grape-juice staining to purple his full lips.

'*"For this must ever be
A secret, kept from all the rest,
Between yourself and me."*'

The Tylers came.

Sir William Withey Gull was committed to St Mary's Hospital, Islington, in the name of Thomas Mason. Was given the number, 124. Nothing more is known. The rumours from here on are all lies. The screams in the night are false theatre. In that decayed zone, hidden on a hilltop, in windblown paper, among hoardings and estate agents, there was no Gull. He was flown.

26

A NAUTILUS INQUISITION.

The Zest of Endurance. Joblard splits in the uneven panels
of a long mirror. Pin-ups and moonshot advertisements on
either side of him. He is swallowed in the red pads of the
machine; forced breath. He emerges. Huge thighs enclose him.
He drives free. Dynamic tension expelled with a lion's roar.
He lies upon a board, dragging down a weighted bar. He does
the circuit, swallowing his own air; relishing the new mysteries
of pain.

At this early hour the gym is his. His young son playing with
a blue motorbike, not concerned with these gruntings and
strivings. The massacre of the previous self, the willed annihilation of past histories of accepted limits and boundaries, continues. Thoracic expansion driving out images of repression. Again:
forcing the set weights, the manifested moral obstacles.

The quest is simplified and brought to the scale of this playpen:
the sculpted machines of steel and chrome and leather; their
chains and balances are for use. The studio is in some way
made redundant. The acts are repeated, with no trace, beyond
sweat and the changing body armour. It is not that anything
new emerges – but that old inhibitions are removed.

The skin softens, becomes childlike. Heaving himself from the
floor of London. But the true child, strapped in his buggy, is
much more ancient, intent. He is open to it all, it still flows
through him and around him, no barriers, nothing to keep
out: he is contained.

The father's head split by the mirror; deformed hemispheres. And the back of the child's head above him. And the moon photograph with the text printed on the reverse showing through as a fault, or stain. And the black doorway with the waiting watcher.

I cannot work up the generosity to suffer this; not for the obvious taints and shower-stall risks, but because I prefer other fate games. There is a polarity of risk in this elimination of comfortable flaws that is useful to Joblard: he has decided to Stalinise his personal history, to re-edit the past. It will appear to be whatever he wants it to be.

The flame is high, but new energies are running into him. To be and not to do. The world was defended by what he made and now he has to keep place in it without these weapons. The objects, accretions, the tools of a false magic are abandoned. He is unhoused. Like Nicholas Lane, he wills his absence from the world. He is erased.

But the child, effortlessly, announces his presence, like the first sentence of *Moby Dick*, such apparent simplicity; it is hardly noticed, but it is final. There. And everything changes by it. The Leviathan is fatally marked, invisibly wounded, brought down. The richest fault in time is the least seen. This ancestor, in his striped-bundle, is sleeping. The head nods over, already weighted.

*

At the back of Guy's Hospital, between Newcomen and Snowsfield, at the corner, in Great Maze Pond is a red brick building, coded with roses and with fruits, once a private ward, now a gym.

The sign *"New Outpatients Department"* is still fresh; but that function has already been terminated. Gull's asylum has closed its doors, last refuge of the least pained; they lock their gates to preserve the status of the doctors. Hospitals translate into gymnasia: members only, boxers, bull-workers, narcissists, cruisers. The facilities include steam baths, that alternate their use between the men and the ladies, with profitable confusion: also a bar.

The child is still out; we take our breakfast coffee.

Involuntarily returning to our past, to the fables we construct out of it. On the river. Tooley Street. I once had a job re-labelling cans of condemned Argentine beef. It was one of the few manual tasks at which I excelled. Worked up to a speed that began to alarm the management. The mountain of silver reduced in a few hours to exhibitionist lines with gleaming new wrappers, all ready for the supermarket shelves. The fact that I was helping to put high risk merchandise into the mouths of babes and sucklings in no way inhibited my performance. I liked where I was. Unknown: I fell into the task. Took my breaks on the riverside, saw the city on the far bank, coming up out of the mud, a sediment of its own memory.

Metal detectives probed the foreshore, eyes down. Truant children made rings out of broken stones. The river eliminates itself, heavy with its repeated lies. Montague Druitt, a victim, taken into the fringe of Ripper mythology, found himself here. Self-assassin only. Swimming out, his pockets filled with pebbles.

Joblard again suffers my ramblings, graciously. A surface calm of near collapse: he checks the sleeper.

'The hospital, that theatre, contains its secret history in its bland outward architecture. The forecourts, quadrangles, iron gates and chapels disguising frenzy and fear. You know that it was founded by a bookseller who made his money speculating in South Sea stocks? The nervous occultism of the merchant again: trading in invisibles. The walls are calcined books.'

Joblard stretches his long jaw, a yawn of suspicion. His boots no longer tapping under the table. Temporary ease. No scratching. A thumb nail grazing the stubble.

'Lies are the only way of getting at the truth. What we know is so stamped down, walked over, familiar – its power is gone.

We can't just carry on repeating the same myths: until we arrive at a fresh version. An authentic replica of our own making.

We must use what we have been given: go back over the Ripper text, turn each cell of it – until it means something else, something beyond us.

Otherwise we never over-reach our obsessions. We're doomed not to relive the past, but to die into it. To abandon the ambition to keep alive what never was, and what never will be, unless we make it so.

The conspiracy is all with time: those on the fringe of event simply disappear. Like the Kennedy assassination. There are *no* reliable witnesses. A sudden wound releases the unintegrated souls, psychic pus, fear and loathing, spectres of world conspiracy.

It's like your bodybuilding – sorry – weight-training. How I describe you, is made into a lie: you change what you appear to be. You make your past a lie, but you do not eliminate it. Nor the fall to future decay.

I can't believe, therefore, in *anything* I say. I repudiate this disbelief. There is *no* explanation that will redeem the time. And if I undermine the lies I am telling about this, this, *this* moment – I mean that we were never here, this conversation never took place – I am doing no more than re-writing a past that never, in fact, occurred. Disallowing the present. Aborting the future. It shifts, slips through our clumsy hands.

The words cover so many fears: are used to hold those fears back. What we can describe is what is known; and knowable. Words keep out the world. What we cannot describe, we cannot know: or truly want to know. How can we let go of all this and sink through the tremble and shiver of the leaves? The cancelled movements, wiped-over holes, the spaces? Those shapeless trees beyond the window, breaking cloud into bone: not holding back in disbelief.

The saints had a word that could redeem it. A word that I

will not use. It cost them too much. They kept out the world to reach it. I cannot say it, even to transcend this pain. Because that word is tied to everything that cannot be reached and is most desired.'

The set is broken. Nothing remains: no pretence that this is a record of any true dialogue. The gym does exist, but that was another country.

We have gone so fast that we are ahead: we are describing what has not yet happened, and what does not now *need* to happen. We have made arrangements to foreshorten the future.

Always erasure, not exorcism. Exorcism merely confers status on the exorcist: who claims, falsely, that he has the power to unmake. Has tricks to stake the demonic, nail the black heart.

Erasure acts over, is a discretion. Joblard's performance in the warehouse erased itself so that the voices were set free. They wound back the memory of the future.

There is no need to rub out the inscription on the stone, for as soon as it has been read, it fades from before your eyes.

*

We pushed the child out into the air, to release him in the small park at the back of St George the Martyr, Tabard Street. We sat on a bench beneath the spread of a mottled london plane tree. It was raised ground. The wall beyond us was a collage of dates and periods and colours, with sealed doors, set at a custodial height. There was a plaque: "This site was originally the Marshalsea prison made famous by the late Charles Dickens in his well known novel 'Little Dorrit'".

Strength had transferred to the child. We are now drained, witnesses, merely. He held the horns of the buggy and wobbled over the grass, not walking free, nor falling to the ground.

On another bench, under the wall, a man was sitting reading.

We recognised him as the barman from the Wheatsheaf. He did not see us. Head over, stern glasses, trembling; back of his hand wiping his eyes. Not weeping, laughing. The solitary celebrant of such laboriously constructed pathos.

27

FROM THE HILL he watched the people crossing the fields, by tracks and pathways, to secure a good position. There were families with small children who had risen in darkness, milk on the table, a slab of coarse bread in the hand, walked twenty miles and further, to be here. The women in black, none of the men bareheaded, and even the children are hushed, imitating the long faces of their elders.

By the time that the sun climbs out of the plantation the whole length of the road, from the station to the church, is marked out with villagers and country people.

He stands watching them; he might be a blasted tree-stump. No breath in him. Now the train has arrived from the city. Smoke and pomp. Ha! The dignitaries awkward as their own ghosts, creaking in starch, scarcely able to articulate their limbs. The gleaming brass of the coffin. "William Withey Gull, Bt., 1816-1890." He is boxed in oak. He is sealed, no breath upon the varnished wood. But his eyes are open. The business is done. Done justly.

A still morning, painted on glass. Black smoke climbs straight from the train. The hats are pipes, polished in stout. The white candle-wax faces. Gloved hands. Walk humbly, walk on. Lord Justice Lindley, Sir Joseph Lister, Sir Henry Wentworth Acland, Sir James Paget, Serjeant Surgeon to Her Royal Highness, Queen Victoria. Walk side by side, and slowly. Struggle as you climb. Wind out of the station and up the hill towards the village; no eyes for the dull fields. Eyes set on the braided tails of the great black horses. Heroic!

This is no coffin of stones. Gull's eyes are open. At last he looks up, out through the thin fibres of wood, at a clear sky. Justified. England marches to a slow beat. Hearts are slowed. The earth turns slowly. Death furls the branches of the trees.

To the village, the lych-gate of St Michael's church. Gull's leg is crossed, arms over chest, a penguin mockery. Hands pressed together, his own effigy, Knight of Landermere. Features lose all detail: a syphilis of time. He weathers.

The moving procession stretches over the nautical mile from station to church, from bishops and baronets at the grave's edge, through surgeons, gentry, wharfingers on the hill, tradesmen, small farmers, fishermen, poachers and lurchers, to the children on the platform.

The ceremony begins.

From the high ground at Thorpe Hall, Gull watches them carry him to his grave. Sees earth fall over his eyes. He is enclosed, nailed down, weighted. In a vault that is big enough for three men. He is free of his own history.

*

The training began in the private plantation of the Hall. Gull was blind, his back to the window. All the windows painted over with pitch; holding out the star needles, the bride light. Not doctor now, nor patient. Not killer. Nor victim. The house had been in his mind for so many years. Lawns, conservatory, ivy. Flat undecorated front, long windows. Hide it in trees, build up the walls. This is truly nowhere. Gull is the house. That is how he dreamt it. This is what he knew.

The ash of matter, of unsmoked Havanas, powdered his sleeve. All matter is dust. Pulse in his neck. He crosses the floor, blind, eyes trained to see nothing, hand on the cage of ribs, a bird in his chest. Out of time. Cycles of birth occur at margin; decomposing light. His hand on the sill: a glove of white powders, stapled with hair, dissected to vein and fibre. A tide-map of the estuary. An illusion of stillness.

The training began in the private plantation. Choirs of stunted and infertile apple trees were interwoven, Merovingian blood-lines; avenues had been hacked and burnt into this thicket. Brambles, wild thorns, blackberries swollen with sour rain; unpicked, flavourless wart clusters: they surround the orchard. Pig-turned mud. Dark archways; a lattice-work of blades and starlight, a scalping rooftree. Green moulds brushing their stiff corduroys. Lichen bruises on torn skin. The stone of a cracked fountain. They are entangled in a nightmare.

Gull had contrived that certain obstacles should be disguised in this thatched stooping labyrinth. Bend! Or tear open your haircap. There were man-traps, bearpits, mummified, or wrapped figures, chained among the trees. Owl-heads grafted onto the bodies of cats. Trip wires ignited sudden flares.

The coachman and the painter were then blindfolded and set loose, zones of the wood were fired. They ran through their terror, screaming, bumping against trees, clutching at the shapes most likely to wound them. They mutilated themselves – until they learnt to navigate their own fear-traces, to scale down the star map onto a computed ground.

The training continued for many months; now the dark was abstracted, the spine's eye quivering and sure in its judgments. Netley the coachman, and the other one, the painter, were invited to sit in the library, back to back, street plans spread in front of them, arms strapped to a board – so that only the hand and the fingers could stretch, could direct the well-inked pens. They read aloud, in synchronised voice, from a Latin text that they did not understand, while their hysterically sensitized fingers guided the nibs through the highways, Old Montague, Finch Street, Heneage, Chicksand, Hanbury, through alleys, Angel, Green Dragon, Lion, courtyards, through the secret city that Gull's will was enclosing.

He could then allow his own vision to fail. He had no further use for it. His eyes could be burnt to the root, their interference countered. He could be wheeled out, or borne on a litter, stretchered, face upwards, freely, among the stars. Beyond the human, involuntary, down paths of merciless light. Connecting the sparks, a child, joining the numbered dots on his slate to reveal a hidden face. Helpless, like the Old Ones, searching the darkness of memory for their gods.

An attendant, on Gull's unspoken order, wove into his hair the lead weights that fishermen use. His hair was already ash, now twisted into dread; the weights rapping against his stiff collar. The load was imperceptibly increased till his skull tipped and his throat tightened. He was removing himself, by degrees, from the grounded creature: the aggressor, the muck-snuffling beast. His face was forced to the sky, opened. His anatomical skills were tabled to murder all that was not mind.

This has not happened – but as you think it, it is happening. Diseases are the dreams of the body. In our diseases we study our future.

While walking alone in the grounds of the Hall, Gull was seized with paralysis. He did not lose consciousness, but fell on one knee. The servants did not discover much difference in his looks and manners, but he said that he felt another man. He walked away from himself, through the orchard and out of the gate. He subsequently had three epileptiform attacks, from which he rapidly recovered; was suddenly seized with an apoplectic attack, fell into a state of coma, and gradually passed away.

Sir William Withey Gull left behind him £ 344,000, with lands and possessions. An estate unprecedented in the history of medicine.

*

Awaking to sleep, the same dream. His brain had burst, no boundaries. Catatonic. Wax Lazarus. Sleep of initiation. He runs the edge. Lies on the blade. No colour. Moving in lucid patterns, unhindered, through the labyrinth. As if carried on water: the outline of Mary Matfellon.

His dream was the nightmare that Hinton had lived. He absorbed Hinton's death into his own. The nurses noted a foetal light emanating from his navel, a specific fear. He saw the houses slide into dust.

His ghost, between a drowned consciousness and the tree, frosts the window. His swollen bearded length covers the branches. Dead breath on the glassed skin: imageless. A yew dripping with earth. The years are wands. Wet clay on his varnished boots.

At night the weight moves from his throat across the damp grass, and above it, a chain of righteousness. The unpeopled garden. Drooping stocks and heavy lidded plants concealing their cannibal instincts.

Himself. Facing himself. Looking in. Looking at. And without pity.

*

No longer Gull, nor Hinton. No longer contained by those descriptions. A table of fish. It is his mother, unharmed, loading fish from her raised skirts onto the bare table. Shimmering bright water stream. From the bell of her skirts she draws fish. He must swallow this abundance.

He must kill with fish daggers. The fish are weapons to stop the mouths of women. His hand alone would prevent the Dark One from seizing the gentle sisters. *Then cut it off!* The seven daughters, the escaping brides. He is Orion, mover of the unnumbered. What he has to do, he has to meet his mother in Hell. Stop up the mouths of women, they have shattered the jar of secrets.

Now he sleeps, once more outside; his length stretched on the grass. The skin of a heifer, soaked with urine. Blind man turns, twists, looking for the sun's track. Where is his mother?

He spills his semen into the grapes. He is cunning. The white grapes are fat with his seed. From this bowl his mother must eat. The taboo is broken. She will bear his child.

On the eastern horizon the seven stars announce his coming. They are doves, also called suicides. Announcing rain. They guard the Water Door, the place of Entrance. Beware now of the scorpion at your heel.

Is it a fish in his closed hand? Juice, unwholesome stickiness; blood. Gull bleeds between his legs. He is smooth. The third son. Boasting of the death of all wild creatures, performance of sacrifice. He menstruates. He holds a beheaded fish between his thighs. He soaks the grass.

Gull's acts described what he can now dream. He enacted the myth. He rehearsed, but did not perform. Now he is smooth. He is his own mother. Old Star, White Star.

She went through the Water Door, she became the Pleiades.

I will carry my womb to the river. An affinity with Rainbows. Day of sun behind showers. Once again at the White House, the cottages. Over sedge and canal. Among cattle. Water track. In a split of land; face to Horsey, to Hedge-end Island. A path over the water.

I can see the man walk out of the woman. Voiceless, steps onto a beach of tongues, live fish; slides. The dead man walks over. He crosses and does not look back. Under the bow of lights.

When the double departs, there are only three days to live.

The water is become a tent; it climbs above the island, a red mountain, then a sheet, then a sheet of white. And behind the sheet the shadows of his father and his mother; they are making love.

Gull felt in his belly a stirring, a movement, something that he could not name, unknown, too slight to name; unstoppable. A child. Who would not be stopped by any force or blade. Beyond will.

His breath was now the tide. And was held.

28

FEBRUARY 1985, a Friday. It is with ever increasing difficulty that he sustains the illusion of dealing in books; out of Colchester with empty bags, once more down the Clacton road, once more breaking at Weeley and going back into the previous; so many times he has concentrated on that sign, Thorpe-le-Soken. A cold day, settled into its own ambiguities. Everything beyond the road has been cancelled.

He begins to understand, in dread, that beneath *this* text also is an uninvited shape, denying his notional control; a snake with two heads that he is straining to force together, venomous fangs bared.

He takes the left hand path and settles for the Crown Hotel. A guinness and a cheap cigar, red notebook stays in my pocket. I don't invoke the "MANAC" anagram which has just occurred to me, "JACKS MEN CAME." It is no solution.

The eyes avoid you; they stare at your knees and hands. No room here for irregulars. Threat spreads over the tiles like a blood stain.

A clatter of wheels and hammers inside the fruit-machine. See the purple grapes spin with the pears. "Across the Pleiades". That is the name of the machine. A farm worker, in suede boots, tries to pull its arm out from the socket.

Now the church has gone, the village street, the pub itself. Painted out in a sudden snowfall. Wind from the steppes decodes the stone, hoods the vicious impact of time. It is shifting, uncertain: dangerous.

I have an appointment in Ipswich and I will not abandon it.

The lanes close on me; skidding, wheel spin, not my decision. The short journey stretches as the light dies. No other traffic on this back road. The sky has fallen into the fields.

The car fails. Unable to climb. The tracks away to the side are walled with drifts. Where I am is nowhere and I have been brought to it, beyond choice. I walk to the top of the hill in leaking shoes, unprepared. Risk insinuates, absorbing the warmth of the known.

A road sign: I beat off the snow, Ramsey. This is truly nowhere and I have arrived.

*

And again, driving in; the sign remains, but the road is never the same. No pretence at bookdealing; I am here simply to be here. And, of course, it is right, it is Michaelmas, the Rector seems to be waiting in the church porch. It is their special festival, feast of St Michael.

This man is both clown and messenger. In his long black skirts he crows around me, on all sides at once, showing off what he has assembled: photographs, lists, old books, cushions, old anything, extensions of his unfocused enthusiasm.

He produces Fred Kempster, the Essex Giant, shaking hands with a woman at an upstairs window of the Bell. The Gull family tree is bannered across the north wall. He shows me the Gull window, fired by the setting sun. St Luke, St John, and Christ, together with what he calls "healing episodes from the gospels." Rituals of obscure transformation.

But he will not allow me to look; always at my elbow, interpreting everything that I am *not* interested in. I must return. Tomorrow. The exhibition will be opened to the public, fully hung. He points out the stone carvings on the arches and around the pillars; fruits of the earth, acorns, poisoned berries and bunches of grapes.

I have to stay overnight, to willingly enter the fictions of M. R. James. There is a room at the Bell. Low-ceilinged, windows opening onto the graveyard. Out over the leaning tombstones, the moss and ivy, to the burial place of the Gulls.

"What doth the Lord require of thee, but to do justly, and to love mercy, and to walk humbly with thy God?"

Not a question, but a statement. Long shadows enlarge the monuments. Narrow the fear into my camera; I sit at the window, letting it come to me through the safety of the lens. The beams of the room creak like a whaler, pipes whistle, the light decays but remains benevolent; it is lived through.

*

The church exhibition will not be open until eleven o'clock and so I decide to walk out of Thorpe to try and discover the Gull family cottage at Landermere Quay.

A heavy sea-fret walks with me, liquid voices. A heightened perception of the trivial throws up from the roadside such named dwellings as "Golden Dawn" and "Wolverine Cottages." But these are soon left behind. There is nothing to guide me but instinct.

Thorpe Lodge is shapeless, soft, gone back. A road turns away for Kirby-le-Soken. I pass it. Cattle in the sea, snorting and stamping, unseen. The sea has rolled over these flat lands: walk under.

Another track, and I do break from the road. A farm building; I turn again. Over a stile and out among the fields. Wet branches soak me as I brush against them. Beaded veils. Glistening webs on the oak. It stops me. I take out the camera and wipe the lens. But this is not the photograph. The field below.

There is the foreshortened outline of something like an up-turned shed. I move down towards it, slithering on the mud slope. It is the shell of a great barge. Burnt out, charred, flaking; beams broken and twisted, grounded. In this drowned field, where water runs out, at this boundary, on the edge of things, between past and future. A spar goes down into the black silt, umbilical, connecting the hulk to this place. It is split, it is half of something.

I recognise it. And know that I have to write my way back towards this moment. This is given. To release my wife from her dreams of minatory buildings, a wind-invaded house, long corridors of strangers: I will return with my family; and my children will climb up onto the wreck, will stand at that rudder. And the connection will be made, the circuit completed.

ACKNOWLEDGMENTS

White Chappell, Scarlet Tracings closes the triad begun with *Lud Heat* (1975) and *Suicide Bridge* (1979): it opens, hopefully, a second triad.

The letter from Douglas Oliver was written in response to *Suicide Bridge* and is published here with his permission.

Sub-texts have been cannibalised from many sources; some are obvious, some obscure. This is not the place to list them.

The contemporary characters represented in this book are, of course, fictional; though invented more by themselves than by the supposed author.

The Victorian characters lived under the names that I have given them: their behaviour is dictated by sources other than historical record.

Also by Iain Sinclair and available from Granta Books:

Lud Heat and Suicide Bridge

'A wonderful poem' Peter Ackroyd

'*Lud Heat* combines research into the sinister dotted lines which link up the Hawksmoor churches of East London – complete with a very fine diagram displaying the pentacles and triangulations which connect churches to plague pits to the sites of the notorious Whitechapel and Ratclyffe Highway murders – with a broken sequence of breathtakingly lovely modern free-verse lyrics.' Jenny Turner, *London Review of Books*

Radon Daughters

'I suspect Iain Sinclair is a genuis . . . he can outgun virtually any writer in England.' John Walsh, *Independent*

'Sinclair is an authentic visionary. Only at the end of the book, however, do we realize we've also been in the power of a genuine wizard, someone capable of tracing patterns and designs only barely perceptible to most people and, more to the point, able to reveal them to us.' Michael Moorcock

Lights Out for the Territory

'This amazing book crackles and fizzes with electricity.' Ruth Rendell

'Anyone who cares about English prose cares about Iain Sinclair, a demented magus of the sentence . . . He is a sublime archaeologist of the present, and his dig has produced one of the most remarkable books ever written on London.' James Wood, *Guardian*